a vacation on the

island

of ex-boyfriends

stacy bierlein

a vacation on the
island
of ex-boyfriends

stories

stacy bierlein

ELEPHANT
ROCK
BOOKS

Published by
Elephant Rock Books
Ashford, Conneticut
www.erpmedia.net/books

First Edition
10 9 8 7 6 5 4 3 2 1

Library of Congress Control Number: 2011937009

ISBN: 9780615529776

Book Design: Melissa C. Lucar

Cover Photo: © Image Source/Corbis
Author Photo: Elisa Tobin

Printed in the United States of America

For my girlfriends,
who never fail to bring wisdom and laughter to the journey

CONTENTS

a vacation on the
island
of ex-boyfriends

stacy bierlein

A Vacation on the Island of Ex-Boyfriends

In three days we have played, cried, ran, fought, laughed, danced, and built fires with them all—every man we've ever wanted. We're exhausted.

The day the ferry left us at this so-called paradise, it looked deserted, until we saw them, lined up on the beach in chronological order. Holy fuck, we said, at the same time. What the hell, we said. Tammi laughed. I didn't. I caught my breath and said, Can I vote them off, one at a time?

Why would you want to do a thing like that? Tammi said, smiling, giving her exes a Miss America wave. They waved back, in sync like line dancers, tanned, goober smiles and wide eyes. Mine looked down at their feet, kicked at the sand. Some whispered hellos. It's going to be a long day, I said. And all this time, I thought we were traveling to Nantucket.

We have to build huts for you, Ben Wexley reported. He held up a copy of *The Complete Idiot's Guide to Thatched Hut Construction*. Ben had spent time on the island before—a lot of women called him ex. At Colgate, we'd called him Tammi's Hunk of Burning Love.

Thanks, we'll build our own, I said.

Don't be ridiculous, Tammi said. Ben smiled.

Let them do it. She winked. Island rules.

So Tammi's ex-boyfriends fell over themselves that first day, flexing muscles, calling her name, fighting for attention, striving to give her shelter. Mine went about the task at a more normal pace, some of them humming, most with their eyes closed. Tammi's hut was going to look like something from a travel brochure for the Four Seasons Maldives. Mine was going to look like a Cub Scout troop experiment.

Are you sure you didn't know about this? I asked her then. An unusually cruel joke, if you did. *Helloooo*, she said, if I had known, don't you think we would have had our roots done?

At the end of that first day I see Michael and I can't believe it. He's on the beach, staring at his feet, watching sand sift between his toes. He hadn't been in the line-up when we arrived.

I march over to him, lift his chin with my forefinger. What are you doing here? His eyes sparkle. Damn his sparkling eyes. You're not an ex-boyfriend, I remind him.

Well, he says, according to the rules of the island, I am. They think I got to you, confused you. That counts.

You didn't get to me, I say. You didn't. Not at all.

Obviously I did, Michael says, a little too smug. Or I wouldn't be here.

Who makes these rules?

I'm not exactly sure, he says, reaching for my hand. According to the ferry operator, what you and I had was called *an emotional affair*.

Well, I say, pulling away. That's wrong. It was just a thing.

Yeah, a thing, he says. A total thing.

He stares and I lighten a little. He has big eyes, green lakes. I look into them too long. It's like he's trying to hold me there, which makes me nervous.

Six months ago, the morning after I slept with Michael, I called Tammi at work. I shouldn't have had those after dinner drinks, I told her. I felt too emotional with him, too attached. He must have thought it was really freaky.

Don't worry about a thing, Tammi advised me. Guys love freaky chicks.

Later in the week, Tammi and I skip the beach and go hiking in the woods. We're still arguing about how we got here. We're never using your travel agent again, I tell her. We push foliage gently aside as we go. Our boots crunch against the path.

The hiking trail narrows so I walk ahead, palming birch barks for balance. The damp smell of moss surrounds us. It's so quiet back here, I say, so great and green.

Tammi sighs. I think she misses them, those past boys on the present beach.

Our path widens a little. We hear walking, crackling leaves up ahead.

I look hard at Tammi. Is that someone looking for you?

I didn't plan a rendezvous back here, she says. I swear. Everyone I've ever, you know, is back at the beach.

The boyfriends are at the ocean, doing the same things they've been doing for days: Tammi's hoot and cheer. They're hot, shellacked in sweat, ready to jump, deep into volleyball competition. Mine sit alone on bamboo mats, scattered and silent, reading and scratching their heads. Jacob and Emil, drunk, play cards and sing fraternity songs. Timothy grips his race form, bitches about his bookie. Johnny, stoned, stands in the waves, twirling a basketball on his finger.

Really Tammi and I only needed one hut. We leave the nightly beach parties together, a bottle of red wine in tow, and talk in one of our huts until we fall asleep. We're amused by the idea that exes out looking for one of us may find an empty hut and think we're hooking up with another ex. And if they spy us in a hut together, drinking wine while snuggled into a sleeping bag, they might wonder if we really like men at all.

Of course, every night we're talking about them. I tell Tammi that some of my exes said *rubbers* and some said *condoms*. I tended to fall harder for the ones who said *condoms*.

A quick glimpse into my chronology: Kyle was high school in Boston—two years of puppy love until the dog fell for my sister. Mitch replaced Kyle and knew a lot more. Geoff was my first college boyfriend. He washed, ironed, and lavender-misted his sheets everyday—the only guy in a Colgate dorm who owned an ironing board.

Eric studied on an ROTC scholarship—my *Officer and a Gentleman* fantasy. Johnny smoked too much, said he loved me nearly as much as weed and 'shrooms. Jacob couldn't keep it up, but could—it turned out—play naked Twister with my roommate while I took exams.

James. Well, for a long time, I was obsessed.

Emil insisted we learn golf together. He was so bad that I'd whiff the ball just to make him feel better. Then he tried cooking classes. Everything he served our friends left them in gas pain.

Marcel had two million frequent flyer miles. He said, Let's go to Australia. I said, Let's start slow. So we went to New York. After MOMA, the Met, and the Guggenheim, he stopped in Central Park, took a deep breath and said, *I like art*.

And? I said.

Huh? he said.

That's it, I said, you like art? We've spent an entire weekend viewing all kinds of exhibitions and all you have to say is, *I like art?*

Yep, he said. That's it. And it was.

Laurence and Brad were one-night stands that lingered for weeks. Timothy wanted to plan our wedding on the third date. You don't even know me, I said. He screwed up his face then, as if I'd said something out of context. Kevin always wanted us to spend weekends with his relatives Chicago. Eventually I snapped out of my lust-haze and dumped him two blocks north of Division Street.

Max didn't enjoy sex unless I agreed to keep repeating after him, Whose dick is this? Whose dick is this? I made the mistake of complaining to Tammi and her then-boyfriend, Rico. All through dinner that night, Tammi and Rico kept saying, Whose fork is this? Whose bread is this? Excuse me, whose wine glass is this?

Samuel stormed out of Einstein's Bagels one day, said, Anna, the hard truth is, you're never going to be a Libertarian. Glen wore turtlenecks and started our first two dates with a detailed defense of his decision to remain uncircumcised. I woke one morning to Anton shaking his head, holding a tape measure over my face, measuring the length and width of my nose, the space between my eyebrows.

On my birthday, Cal asked me what flowers I loved. Lilies, I said, irises, orchids. He gave me alstroemarias. They're so practical, he said. My mom likes them. They're sturdy and plain and can get by on little water.

In the woods, as we get closer to the crackling sounds, we see a man, dark curly hair, a moustache. He waits for us to catch up. It's Anna, right? he says, when we're face-to-face. Do you remember me? he asks, quiet-voiced, and it takes me a minute.

David? Oh my God, I say. He's Megan's, I tell Tammi.

David used to be engaged to Megan. He moved out of her house without a word, left behind his clothes and a note that said he wasn't what she needed.

Where is she? I demand. I know she doesn't want to see him.

I step closer to Tammi and out of the path of a darting dragonfly.

I don't know, David says. But we're waiting. We're ready to build her hut.

And out of the trees walk Al, Carson, Jack, and Bo, each taller than I would have imagined. Al carries lumber. Carson wears a set of red curtains over his shoulder. Bo has a rifle. Jack has killed a deer.

Wow, Tammi says, puffing out her lower lip. Then she remembers about Megan.

Megan's boyfriends were so maddening that she wrote tell-all songs about them. Two of her three albums immediately hit the Top Ten. She's dating women now and happy enough that she hasn't recorded an album in years, but the old ones keep selling. Everyone loves a break-up song.

Hey, Tammi says, Megan's ex-boyfriends are hunters!

Well, most of them, Carson says, fingering the red fabric.

Rays of light sift in through trees. Megan's men look anxious. I turn from them and pull Tammi reverse on the path with me, so fast she misses her chance to smile at them, to Miss America wave. They were great looking, she says.

We should get to the dock, I say, give Megan some warning.

Sure enough, as we arrive at the dock, the ferry chugs into view. The sun disappears behind a cloud. Rain sprinkles on us. As the ferry gets closer, I see Megan on board wearing her backpack. We wave our arms at her. I scream her name as hard as I can.

Anna? she yells back, surprised.

It's the Island of Ex-Boyfriends, I scream. I saw David.

What? she yells. She's leaning over the ferry's railing, trying to hear over the chugging.

David, I scream, but my voice starts to give out.

David is here, Tammi yells. With that Megan drops her pack, runs to the front of the ferry and into the pilothouse. We see her pulling the ferry operator to the bow. Suddenly his body arcs above the railing; he goes head first into the water.

Moments later the ferry makes an about-face, turns with the speed and ease of a Porsche. The operator surfaces, screams *hey, hey*, then swims for our shore.

Thank God, I start to say, then I realize…

We're stuck here, Tammi says, but she fails to sound disappointed. What Megan couldn't have known, what we've only recently figured out—the ferry is the only way off the island. As water swells up around it, the ferry glides toward the horizon.

The rain stops and we walk back to the main beach and round up our boyfriends to tell them this so-called vacation may last a little longer than expected. Some of them don't mind—Rico, in fact, starts jumping up and down—but others look annoyed. Nice move, Anna, Emil says. Mitch, Jacob, Timothy, and Cal screw up their faces.

Ben Wexly looks at the sky, grunts. In all the times he's spent here, nothing like this has ever happened. You're still such a pain in the ass, Tammi tells Ben.

Tammi stands next to me, looks away from the crowd. Her attention divides. She's trying to decide how to get an invitation to Megan's boyfriends. She's planning a barbeque.

Thanks a lot, Johnny whines. He's the most annoyed. We don't have to look at him to know it. He's running low on weed. He coughs, says, That's just great.

Give her a break, Michael says, stepping out of the crowd. This stops everyone.

Tammi nudges me. Michael smiles; walks toward me. His hair has curled more since he has been here. His board shorts are as green as his eyes; his chest is burning.

He reaches for my hand. The other boyfriends look confused. Tammi beams.

I told you guys love freaky chicks, she whispers.

Michael leads me to the quiet part of the beach. We walk in wet sand. My hiking boots leave imprints that waves will fill with water. He squeezes my hand extra hard.

We hear Tammi and the others cheer in the background. Volleyball games continue.

An interesting bunch of guys back there, he says, and raises his left brow. He can't imagine me with any of them. And they all seem like a long time ago, even here.

I'm confused, I tell him. It is so very confusing, I think, traveling this close to his skin.

I hear Tammi's cheer again, and I think hey, she's not playing volleyball—she's cheering for me. We stop walking and Michael faces me. He hasn't shaved. I feel clunky in these hiking shorts, these boots. I have way too much clothing on my body and want it to melt away.

I wonder, he says. His words are more even now, more careful. He smells like Coppertone. What? I ask. My hands are shaking. Why in the world are my hands shaking?

I wonder if we could make it, he whispers.

Ugh. What do you mean? I say. If I'd wanted to speak in riddles for the rest of my life, I could have stayed with Cal or Mitch or Johnny.

The thing is... he begins. He squints his eyes. He puts both hands on my face.

What do you mean exactly? I want to know.

He moves toward me, in that slow way, in that soap opera way I dreamed about as a teenager, the way that says, I'm going to kiss the freaky chick before the next commercial break.

I put my hands on his chest. I don't even think about it—it's automatic. I don't know where my hands are until I feel his heartbeat in my fingers. He turns and points to the horizon. I think we could make it, he whispers. He turns back to me and moves his lips even closer to mine. I feel his air, his breath.

I think we could make it, he says, with a slow and careful swim.

Luxor

Once you hear the sound of gunfire, you will always recognize the way the blasts slice through the air. When you dream of a child running into your arms, you will always recall the moment when her small body melts into yours, her small arms curl around your neck, and your arms fall over her like a blanket, clinging to all the warmth inside. Once you photograph the Nile, you understand how it is that this great river never fails to flood its banks.

Hundreds of people scream and fall as the first shots slice into the air. She is lost from her parents and yelling and turning as people dive to the ground around her. I leave my camera bag on the dirt and run toward her, holding my arms out. She runs into them, and I charge forward, clinging to her, pushing both our bodies down behind a short block wall. All I can think is *shelter her. Find shelter.* On the other side of the wall, a tour bus stops in the distance.

We tremble behind sandstone blocks. I cannot determine the directions of the shots. In Egypt, there is so much sky.

Across the path, a woman selling hats freezes in gesture. It all happens so fast. It all happens so slow.

LUXOR, Egypt. November 17. Gunmen burst into the courtyard of Hatshepsut's Temple this morning and battled police for more than three hours. Egypt's government believes at least 70 people dead, ten Egyptians. The Swiss Foreign Ministry reports 20 Swiss tourists missing. Several British tourists are also missing. An American woman, said to have been photographing the 3,400 year old temple, is presumed dead.

Later it will occur to me that a good photographer would have never left her camera. She says *Arretez!* into the air, toward the blasts. I loosen the girl's grip on my waist, but continue to hold her tight. Blasts come again and again and again and I can no longer see. Sand and dirt rise around us and her *arretezs* become whispers. She hears my fear.

She cries into my shirt, and I know nothing to say that can calm her; no way to explain the bullets. She is four, maybe five, wearing a blue dress and Elmo sneakers. Her beautiful brown hair has fallen out of a ponytail. Her parents must be near. Even in this terror, I envy them. Sometimes our hearts might break down, but they just break open. This is how the doctor described me: My womb is a hostile environment.

Over the shots I hear a man's voice yell Mimi! *Attention*, Mimi! Then a woman's voice, crying, yells the same. *Maman*, she screams, and I hear her mother's cry.

I have your daughter in my arms, I yell.

We're safe, I say. For now, I think.

I try to calm my mind enough to say this in French, to yell it out so her parents understand. We are laying on the ground, Mimi half under my chest, my arms around her. I can see nothing through clouds of smoke and sand.

Thank you, the woman yells in English. *Bless you*, she sobs.

I do not run toward their voices, and they do not run to mine. We lie in the sand knowing we may not outrun death.

It seems amazing, the things that dart into your mind when death startles everything around you. On safari, travelers learn the gestation periods of animals. For the zebra it is twelve months, sixteen for the white rhino, three for the lion, three and a half for the leopard, fourteen for a giraffe. For the elephant it is nearly two years—twenty-two months to be exact. Six months for baboons. The nine months that I could not give to forming a life, I try to give to discovering Africa.

I want to learn the rules of the wild. I want to accept my limitations. Baboons have a highly developed social structure. Last night there was an old moon, a waning moon. I am a non-breeder. I am the tip of the branch on the tree of my ancestry. Travelers take well water to the Nile. How strange it is to be held in awe by a river and forbidden to drink its water.

Before the blast, an English-speaking guide told his group, *the name Hatshepsut means she whom…*. And it sounded like he said, *a moon embraces*. But it must have been *Ahmose embraces*. Ahmose is the mother of Hatshepsut, and she also ruled Egypt. But I like it the way I heard it—she whom a moon embraces. Native Americans believed the moon was a single woman living near the sun. The block we hide behind is like the stones that built this temple.

A piece of earth shatters nearby, and we hold our heads down.

It's okay, I tell her.

We'll be fine, I lie.

I remember a poem that calls on the moon and asks her to pity the writer and drench her in loneliness. I assumed she was lonely without a man, but no. The poem meant lonely without child. When I was little I announced to my mother that I would run away to Egypt.

Egypt, she laughed. Do you know what they do to girls in Egypt? In Egypt, girls are nothing.

En route to Africa it hit me. As a young girl planning my future, I wanted to run away to the past. And what I can't think, and what I can't stop thinking, is that I will die here in the past.

A mother must have some heroic qualities about herself, and she must release them at the right moment. There seems no way to prepare for this. A woman must find her own way; be strong, then act. Queen Hatshepsut had one child, a daughter. Her successor deleted their names from all documents and ceremonies. Hatshepsut spent most of her life trying to prove her rule God-given. She cross-dressed lavishly; she wore ceremonial beards. Shots sound from all directions, random places.

Pregnant mothers automatically stroke their bellies, practicing for when the baby is born, trying to send energy, or take away fear. *Welcome in Egypt*, people call at the airport. Outside the airport you see bicycles everywhere, with little bells. Men eat dates and figs from brown paper bags. Temples are tombs. The little girl in my arms will not stop crying, and I would never tell her to.

It's true that terror jumbles thoughts together. I am not ready to fall away and die. As a teenager, fighting with my mother, I would say, I will never do this to my daughter. To which my mother would laugh and say, You will never have a daughter. You are too selfish and lazy to be a mother.

In front of this temple, I thought of the child I wanted to have, and not the men with whom I tried.

Textbooks make Egyptians white, but really they are the most beautiful shade of brown. My hunger to love is not always attractive. I was pregnant for two months, then three. Camels are fed dates.

It's okay, I keep telling Mimi. I don't know what else to say. The obvious; *I'd do anything to keep you alive.*

I think they must tire soon, of the shooting back and forth, but I have no experience to back this up. They must run out of bullets or something. *Something.* Mimi stops trembling but continues to cry, and I try to look at my watch—they have been shooting so long—but I don't want my arm to leave her body. I hold her and protect her and wish she were my own, even in this.

Je m'appelle Deena, I tell her. As soon as it is safe, we will find your *maman*.

Enshahallah, I say. It is the first Arabic word I learned. God willing. Dust and heat and fear burn up my sides.

Let's think about pyramids, I whisper to her, how grand they are.

So close to death and I know I could hold this child forever.

When this is over, I will call my best friend; tell her that I am alive. If the gunfire here has been reported, Leigh will have heard it from Richard, her fiancé, who works at CNN. She will have called my hotel room in Cairo. She will have called my mother, then our friends, and will have driven a semi-circle on Atlanta's I-285 to hold vigil in Richard's office, to get the news as it comes through. Leigh will know more of the event that I do, here in the danger of it. She will think that the world is too big and too small at the same time. She knows how my life works; that somehow, I will have been in the thick of it. She will assume the worst.

Leigh and I grew up with stories of mummy curses and legends of discovering ruins. I let myself notice, only for a moment, the heat of the sun and the guns; the ground burning. In Africa, the sun drops itself like a weight. Mimi's heart beats strong; it pounds into my shoulder.

How grand they are, Mimi. She nods gently.

Yes, I say. The pyramids are wondrous, like the beats of her heart.

We do not rise from the ground until others do; until there are medics aboard the nearby tour bus. Until we hear her parents' voices again. I stand slowly, with Mimi in my arms, and wipe dirt from her face. Her face is streaked by hot tears, and we both take deep, tiring breaths. I turn away from the tour bus, so that she won't see the blood stained on its side. A man and a woman run toward us. *Mimi! Mimi!* She jumps away and runs into her mother's arms. Mimi's mother lifts her and her arms curl around her mother's neck.

Their chests melt together. Mimi's father, tall and brown, pulls me into his arms, crying, saying over and over, *merci. Merci, merci.* Medics run past looking for the wounded. He tells me that maybe I have saved his daughter, and I want to tell him that maybe she has saved me. At the time I am too shaken-up to know that I will always feel the way she held onto me. The sand will always be in our hair, the ringing always in our ears.

Where It Starts

The ocean view room in Santa Monica had been her idea, but the relentless afternoon sun flooded their bed now, hot and unforgiving. He had thrown off his clothes fast and fallen back onto the bed, trying to crack his back while she stood nearby, wiggling out of her skirt. Her quip to Elaine—who also had an older man—was that they would spend twenty-five minutes cracking his back for five minutes of sex. But she didn't care. Her pathetic reality was that she would have spent twenty-five days cracking just about anything for five seconds next to him.

He raised an eyebrow as she climbed on top of him. You're still dressed, he said. She still had on the black bra and thong purchased for the occasion, although she knew he wouldn't really care. He wanted her naked. Still, she wouldn't forsake the ensemble. It was a runway bra, an it-girl bra. He would have freaked if she told him her LaPerla bill might rival their bill for this room.

Only for another moment, she assured him, leaning down to kiss him while reaching back to undo the hooks herself. He had never taken anything off her, expected a woman to do this part on her own. She kissed him the way she always kissed him— as if everything in her life led to this moment. The minute she was free of the excellent bra, he was on top of her, invigorated by her bareness and his newly cracked back. He kissed her hard and they went on like that, fighting for the top, laughing through their kissing when they found themselves on bottom.

This was a fantastic idea, he said. She wasn't sure if he meant the hotel, sex, reuniting, or all of it, but she wrapped her legs around his in agreement. His condo was being heat treated for termites; she had leant her house to a friend shooting a cereal commercial. If only temporarily, this was their place. He kept saying it like that: *Our place*—it has a nice ring to it, doesn't it, honey?

Baby, he kept saying, as she kissed his ears, his neck, the freckles on his shoulders—all parts of him she had missed. He kissed her and touched her with some degree of urgency, refusing to slow down for even a second. He needed things to accelerate, never linger, and so they did. At some point he lost track of the bed; they landed together with a hard thud on the floor. They burst out laughing.

If I were one of your thirty-year-old boyfriends, he said, staring at the ceiling, we'd keep fucking right here on the floor and I'm sure it would be hot. But I'm in my fifties, and I really need to get back into that bed.

She stood up, let the thirty-year-old boyfriends comment slide, knowing it would annoy her when she recalled it later. There were no boyfriends. From the moment she first heard his voice, there had been only him. Even in the time they were broken up, she had viewed every other man through the lens of him. Other men bored her. One year, three screenplays, and two houses later she was back with him, renewed.

They arranged themselves in the bed; she touched his chest while he pulled at the cool sheets. She wanted to say something about being in his arms again after all this time, but that wasn't right exactly. His hold on her had never been a tender one or simply physical. There was no denying that she loved him. She loved him, and how she craved him. She was not as strong as she let her girlfriends believe. It turned out obsession was more powerful than logic or even pride. This time she would do anything to keep him.

She'd been so taken by him from the beginning—lost in the days she spent intoxicated by the sound of his voice—that after the breakup it had been difficult to work. A few weeks later she managed to pick herself up, to write as furiously as she ever had. There was a pathological quality to her drive then. She wrote scripts for films he might see, or at least read about· in the trades—they were still in the same industry after all— and long for the time when they were in it together. If it wasn't a healthy approach, it was one that advanced her career. Her friends described her as heartbroken and functioning.

She had no intention of going back to the heartbroken part. She pressed her body against his. I love you, he said. This time she made herself believe him.

LAX

They stepped off the jetway into a nearly deserted gate area. The smell of the bright blue airport carpet always bothered her, probably the ammonia in the cleaner. She wrinkled her nose. An appropriate end, she thought, to their three-day Seattle disaster.

I'll find my own way home, she said, walking ahead of him.

You cannot be serious, he said.

She stopped, turned back to face him and said, It's over. I cannot be the one doing all the wanting.

He stared at her. That's amazing, he said, and he wasn't being sarcastic. Did you just blurt that out, or have you been thinking it all day? Because it's an amazing line. Beautiful, really.

Cate Blanchett could deliver that line. Kate Winslet or Julia Ormand.

The weekend didn't need to be rehashed. He had hardly cared whether she was with him in Seattle or not, and she wasn't willing to be put aside again. It's my line and I'm serious, she said, breathing deeply as she watched him realize his mistake.

I know, I know, I know, he said, trying to return, shaking his head as if he could shake himself out of his brain. He stepped closer, grabbed her arm, took a deep breath.

Honey, I'm so sorry you feel this way.

She stared back. This was the best he could do—the only sort of apology she would ever receive from him. Not, I'm sorry I made you feel this way. Only, I'm sorry you feel this way. An insistence that her feelings, not his actions, were the burden.

People from their plane hurried around them wheeling carry-ons to the escalator. She had dropped everything at his invitation. One of his clients had a film premiering at the Seattle Film Festival. We'll go to the movie, he promised, and have the rest of the weekend to ourselves. She attended the movie alone, as he spent that night and the following two fighting on the phone with his ex-wife.

Somehow the wounds from our divorce are still very raw for her, he had explained.

I would appreciate it, she said, if those wounds could be described to your voicemail for a few hours so that we might salvage our weekend.

If the call goes to voicemail, she will know you're with me.

Why shouldn't your ex-wife know that I am with you? She literally clenched her fists as she said this.

Honey, please. She is crazy. Knowing this is serious will make her crazier. And that isn't fair to the kids.

I don't want to be a problem for your kids, she whispered, but I want you.

He hadn't responded then because the phone rang again.

And now, in the middle of the airport, he looked at her like she was the crazy one.

Let me make it clear, she said. This is goodbye, and I don't give a fuck which actress says it best on screen.

He didn't chase or fight her, and while she had not expected him to, she walked quickly, knowing the reality of it could crumble her at any minute. Even before she exited the baggage area and found a taxi she felt awful without him. But she felt terrible with him, so either way she was screwed.

West Hollywood

It was late afternoon in a bungalow he had rented for the month to be closer to the studio. She lifted the bedroom window open to feel a soft breeze, to smell the lavender in the yard, WeHo's determined gardens always fighting the smog. They met for lunch at a nearby café and failed to eat a thing, this being their first time, anticipation trumping hunger. They lied atop the duvet now, shirts off, facing each other and beginning the essentially awkward maneuvering out of pants. He slowed down, hesitated to unbutton hers; mumbled something ridiculous about her clothes being too nice to mess up.

She said, I would never have worn something you weren't welcome to rip off me. She got out of her pants herself, pushing them off the bed with her foot. She worked his belt buckle quickly, tugged at his belt, whipping it out of the loops, tossing it to the floor.

Well, he said, actually rolling his eyes. You know you could have just left the belt attached to the jeans. That was all very dramatic, he whispered, but inefficient, actually.

He had a serious but practical look in his eyes. He got on top of her then, but he wasn't playing. He looked seriously annoyed, in fact, that she had separated his jeans from their accessory. She should have suggested a more vibrant use for the belt at that moment, to challenge his nerve, or simply to make it all make sense. But she only wanted to get his jeans off and get on with it.

It had taken them a ridiculously long time to get to this moment. With his business travel, the dozens of evenings devoted to his daughters' soccer and basketball games, and her trips to New York to help care for her ailing grandmother, it was beginning to seem like this relationship might never grow beyond their phone calls.

You're right, she said, because she knew nothing else to say, bothered by his rightness. And it confused her—the inexplicable shift that occurred when the belt hit the floor; the way they were poised more for battle than tenderness. He seemed different now, alone with her, older, suddenly judgmental. She touched his face, needing to impose the real moment quickly over the one she had fantasized.

It hadn't started like this, both of them nervous and annoyed, finally together in an ivory bedroom that would always look more like a set design than a home. He was still wearing his jeans when he went down on her. She finally got it then—that he was a man who needed to conquer a woman long before he loved her.

MANHATTAN BEACH

Often she would convince Elaine and Leigh to go with her to Sunday open houses. While Elaine and Leigh weren't house hunting, they loved disorder. They were endlessly fascinated by the clutter in peoples' cabinets and garages. Classic, Elaine would say, the owners keep their extra shoe laces in a bag next to the waffle iron.

Leigh would make a game of predicting whether the seller had employed a staging company. Stainless steel garage door, she would say, dead giveaway.

They would see familiar faces touring houses, the real

estate groupies. Someday, Elaine warned, before this boom is over, we are going to play hooky from work and go to those Tuesday broker caravans. They're catered, you know.

On a May afternoon in a flimsy rose stucco Mediterranean—there was no excuse, she thought, for a house not to have good bones—she told. Don't kiss and tell is such a lame rule, Elaine agreed, when one has interested girlfriends. And technically, she hadn't kissed him anyway.

It is so refreshing, she said, to be with an actual adult; one who loves his work, admires mine, and can talk about something more than surfing. He's insane, she said. In a way that I like, she added, before Leigh could grow alarmed.

It was disarming, she thought, feeling so close to a man she had never met face to face. She was about to say that she was in love with him, but that sounded ridiculous. He had discussed with her hundreds of things, including living together, yet they had never had an actual date.

Leigh and Elaine exchanged glances.

She worried aloud that he was the king of premature conversation.

Leigh nodded her head as Elaine advised her to sleep with him for real and immediately, to make sure that was the only premature thing.

Ventura

Sometimes there was no pretense of a professional question. There wasn't even a greeting. She picked up her phone and he said, Baby, what are you wearing?

She was curious, amused, and intrigued. She always played along.

A little white camisole, she said, and a miniskirt that I'm wiggling out of right now—I have ten minutes.

The miniskirt was a little lie she allowed herself. Actually she wore Lakers sweatpants, ten years old and worn-through at the knees. The camisole was real, but it was under a Miami Heat tank top. Too often she wore rival teams.

Wiggling is good, he laughed, wiggling is very, very good. So where are you? he said, trying to set the stage. The living room? The bedroom?

The study, she said. She wasn't used to being the kind of woman whose house had a study. It sounded to her like she lived on the damned Clue board. I am Miss Scarlet, she thought, with the candlestick, in the study.

She heard his breathing deepen. Are you going to sit in a chair? Lie on the sofa? No, she said. In an age of mobiles and texts and e-mails, she and Agent Phone Sex—she called him this now, but only in her head—had yet to be in the same room. She had been rehabbing small mid-century houses—living within her projects—between films for years, but never had she encountered a house so quiet. She was not used to this quiet.

Looking around her study, it occurred to her what she really wanted. You're going to fuck me against the bookcase, she said. You stand, facing me. My shoulder blades are pressed into the bookcase; my legs wrapped around your waist. I want your hands grabbing onto my hips; my fingers clutching the shelves harder and harder as you're fucking me.

His breathing became even deeper. Ten points for originality, he said.

She breathed deeper too, relieved. Today she was the Hollywood person getting the ten points she did not deserve. She was stealing from the last movie she rented, James McAvoy fucking Keira Knightley in the library, her head falling back into the spines of Edith Wharton and Henry James.

His breathing and mumbling accelerated. He told her how he wanted her, how fantastic it was going to be in person, how he wanted to hear her to come, needed to; how he wanted her to come hard, never to hold back; to give him everything she had.

But it hadn't started there, gripping the phone in the study of her new Ventura remodel, breathing in fresh paint as she worked her fingers in the exact place she would later want his tongue. It hadn't started with *Atonement*.

He asked her, Baby, are you wet?

She said, Not yet, so keep talking.

SHERMAN OAKS

There was only a moment when she was just a screenwriter and he was just her agent; a moment she failed to remember, the memory taken over by the calls of subsequent weeks when they had yet to meet but talked incessantly about potential film projects. If they were both in town they would spend days on their mobiles while tending to their respective tasks, his car to her car, his club to her gym, his juice bar to hers. It seemed no one in Southern California kept an office anymore. Plus, the gridlock created by construction closures on Los Angeles freeways that spring made coffee dates or quick meals together a near impossibility. You do realize, he teased, if we lived in New York or London, we'd probably be married by now. He loved to hate Los Angeles and every aspect of Hollywood. They would be talking still, or he would be anyway, when they returned to their homes at night.

You've made a good case for Beirut—that probably is the right place to set this film. I mean, what do we care, they'll shoot the whole thing in fucking Toronto anyway. If we get a young director, they'll want to do the gun scene in some Arabic pop nightclub, which will be obnoxious as hell, but we'll deal with it. And really, fuck The Social Network. *What about a film addressing the dangers of the Internet fragmenting society? Yes, I mean fragmenting. The changing landscape of the Southwest— promise me we'll get that into a film in some way that the cinematographers can't fuck up. I mean, have you seen what has happened to Phoenix? What the hell? No, no, no, you are not*

23

writing about Tibet again. My head will explode. Another love affair with Buddhism? Jesus Christ. What more can Hollywood possibly say about the Dalai Lama? What do people even give a shit about these days? 9/11 doesn't sell anymore, which pisses me off. The vampire and zombie shit is over—thank fucking God. Diets. As if we didn't get enough of this calorie counting crap in the 80's. Goddamned diets are everywhere, but that's hardly useful to us. No one is buying a film about the fucking Zone, that's for sure.

They switched to land lines and phone sex whenever it occurred to him to worry about brain damage.

The way we are together, it's exciting, isn't it baby? I like the way we're beginning, he said, his voice slower, relaxed now. When I have an idea, you are the very first person I want to talk to. We connect so easily. We focus so well. I promise you, I'll be a calming factor in your life. You know, someday soon you will want to quit this house-flipping obsession and move in with me. Listen, we want the same things. We actually make sense.

She liked and feared that his mind was always ahead of hers, no negotiations, he and she all over the map, already a *we*. He was so sure of everything, his questions never really questions.

Okay, baby, what are you wearing?

WHERE THE I-10 MEETS THE 405

Please, please tell me you did not sign with CAA, Leigh said.

Her friend Leigh had called like she always did, from her car during a commute, filling those dead minutes of gridlock and the heat of morning sun at the juncture. She answered Leigh's call half awake in her kitchen, where she had forced herself to make coffee, trying to get writing time in before the drywall guy arrived.

I met a really impressive agent at the premier last night, Leigh continued. Not ICM—he's a lone gun. I sung your praises and gave him your number without missing a beat. Oh yes, I'm serious. He's going to call you tonight.

Leigh took a deep breath. And you're going to love him.

Linguistics

I t is three o'clock in Prague. I'm lying in a dark room in a
white hotel bed under a large and gorgeous man from Croatia.
Tomorrow—well, today, actually—is June 22nd, Summer
Solstice, the longest day of the year. And I can think of no better
way to spend it than twisted in these sweating sheets with a
beautiful man I cannot understand.

My hands grip his shoulders as he whispers in my ear.
I soften under the sound of his voice, trust him immediately.
He speaks little English, we speak little Czech, and I speak no
Croatian. I've come once, from his tongue. I've left teeth marks
around every notch of his spine, and he, in return, has pushed his
teeth into my shoulder, not meaning to draw blood, but drawing
and tasting it anyway. He tastes my skin, every inch of me. My
desire has never been so fast and persistent. We are the Museum
of 3 a.m., a gallery of body fluids.

Alen, I say. His name is Alen.

I come three times more before daylight. We move in
flowing knots, no longer sure where one body ends and the other

begins. We explore, giggle, quiver, and this is the language we speak: hands, mouths, eyes, ears, tongues, toes, thighs, teeth.

Ten percent of the world's languages put the verb first, use action before meaning. As we come together he cries, looks deep into my eyes, runs his fingertips across my face.

This is how we got here:

I notice him the moment he walks into Allegro. The waiter points him to the table next to mine. He smiles to me as he takes his seat. The room, filled with yellow tablecloths and orange chairs, seems to grow even brighter around us. He looks a look that invites me to look back, and my face heats with the way it seems so essential and ridiculous at the same time—the staring and blushing, looking and wanting.

His eyes are brown, soft like a little boy's, at odds with the lines around them. His face is hard, his cheekbones high. He smiles as if he is about to say something incredible, but doesn't say a word. Just his smile, there, in space.

Finally, he looks to the newspaper on my table, its front page a series of maps of the Balkans. I hand the paper to him. Would you like?

No, he says. I know already. I am here to forget.

Yes, I say. Our smiles go for a moment. We look away, look back. Evening light disappears, so waiters pull curtains, bring candles. Excitement huddles in my stomach, new, a contrast to all the feelings before it.

My father died six weeks ago.

For weeks I've been numb from crying, chaos, feeling that I've been kicked hard in the chest, then just staring into the shock of it. When I made myself go to work, I stared at my office door, dreaming my father would walk through it at any moment. He'd notice my swollen eyes, the red lines burned into my cheeks by tears, and say *No, no! Look! Here I am.* As if I could press rewind, and he would come back.

So I decided to go, leave my cruel dream behind. I quit my job as a researcher, planned this month in Prague, then a month in London.

He'd want you to do something more responsible with his money, Rodney told me. Rodney and I had parted years before, and still he spoke as if we were a couple. He was never the right man for me, but not exactly the wrong man either.

I just can't do this anymore, I said, this expansiveness. Even the crowded freeway looks like loneliness. Rodney shook his head, told me to go slow, just wait.

No, I said, refusing to back down. My father would want me to live.

So I'm here in the Czech Republic, saying yes to a beautiful man from a war-torn home as he gives up his own table, brings a bottle of wine to mine. His voice soothes me as we try to talk. We laugh as we stumble through phrases. Before we've finished our first glass, my mind is everywhere, wanting his hand to reach for mine, imagining him inside me.

His smile appears again, wider. He seems on the verge of something, again says nothing at all. This leaves me nervous in all the right ways. When finally he reaches for my fingers, I feel lighter, drugged. My body moves closer and closer to his, and there is no turning back. We will leave the restaurant together. His lips will brush against mine. This is exactly what I need—to be shaken up and rearranged.

We go to my room, find the bed turned down, daisies left on the pillows. The bedside lamps are dimmed, and I laugh, because it seems, for a moment, more like a stage play than my life. I lock the door and turn to Alen. His lips touch my shoulder and we cannot wait. Alen gasps when I bite first, then smiles, relieved. We are biters.

With our teeth, we grip each other's skin, leave maps. Lovebites, scratchmarks. Longer bites leave little bruises, beautiful splatters of purple or blue. My heart races when I see his imprints on me. His tongue leads the way to the next place. The human body can take more than we think. Alen has known me for one evening, yet understands well—I am not made of glass.

Scholars say half the world's languages will be extinct in the next century. It seems so wrong, I think, the way everything in this world can disappear. Cultures, parents, systems of words. So this is how Alen and I hang on. We pull at each other's hips, lean our faces toward one another's shoulders, grab this moment, sink our teeth in.

In the morning we cannot make ourselves dress. It seems all wrong to wear clothes in his presence. We talk, giggle, many of our words just sound, soft music.

He learned Russian when he was young, some English from American songs. I took French in college, learned pieces of Spanish growing up in San Diego. Alen and I try new words, bite in new places. We feel, stare. *Uho*, ear, *usta*, mouth. *Stomak*. We hold each other's gaze. Our cravings persist, and we bite into each other's arms, fall into sex all over again.

Housekeeping comes to the door, and I say No, not yet, please, we need more time. Thank you, they mumble. More time, they repeat. The fortunes of languages are bound up with those of its speakers. This new language we've found—we want to learn more, to memorize.

Prague's famous bridge is lined with statues. Near the center sits a statue of the nun St. Luitgard in the middle of a vision. People call her the finest sculpture in the Czech Republic.

Prince Charles claims to adore her, and pledged money to save her before the elements wipe the look of wonder from her face.

High from hours of touch, Alen and I look to our clothes scrambled in piles on the floor, agree we must try to rejoin the outside world. He will go, he nods. He writes, *Staromestska restaurace 20:00* on the notepad by the phone.

I smile, nod. He begins to button his shirt and cannot finish the job without his mouth on mine, our tongues twisting together, bodies trembling to the floor. He is over me, looking into my eyes. His breath fills me, brings back the pounding in my chest. I move to the top and he grabs my ass as I bite into his chest. *Da*, he says, yes.

After, he showers, tries to dress again. His hair is damp, thick, framing his square jawline, his expression more intense than before. This time it is me who cannot bear his going. He cannot walk out that door, I think. I cannot let him go.

He completes the buttoning of his shirt, pulls on his pants and shoes. Then he is at the door, his right hand on the knob, my mouth is on his, his left hand on my neck, then both of his hands in my hair, pulling, needing.

He bites my earlobe, groans. I put my hands on his pants, and impossibly, yes. I pull away, drop to my knees, undo his pants, take his penis in my mouth. My lips grip on for dear life and in this way I ask him to stay.

Soon we are against the door, then the wall. I am atop the desk, he is standing, my legs are around his waist. He cries out when he comes, throws his body over mine like a blanket. *Hvala*, he says. His eyes shine with all of it. I am saving him from something the way he is saving me.

We move onto the bed and into another night. We wear hotel robes until the room service man appears. We sit in bed, the sheets forming little hills around us as we eat salad, rolls, crepes, drink wine. We watch each other, smile. It feels good, strange, to smile. But I don't need to articulate any of this. It seems Alen knows everything.

After dinner, Alen finds his jacket, takes his train ticket from the pocket and my flight itinerary from the desk. He mimes tearing them up into little pieces, dropping them across the room like confetti. We laugh like drunks, hold each other again. I feel my heart beating, the muscles around my mouth aching. Our previous plans like dust on the rug. Now there is only Prague, this bed, our teeth sinking into flesh. *Make love to me right now. Make me love the right now.*

Two weeks. In daylight we go to Pruhonice, Sedlac, and Koneprusy Caves. At night we make love in facing, half-facing, and matrimonial positions. Our tongues skim each other's lips. He breaths hot air over me, slips his fingers inside me, makes me call out and rise up. Birdsong at morning. Little death.

This is what I know about him: enough.

We walk Charles Bridge in the mornings and notice how clouds seem to arrange themselves perfectly around it. We look to the stone and brick path ahead, the water sparking below. Like the teenagers around us, we stop to make out at various places. Sometimes we are silly, playful, laughing with the crowds around us. Other times, we rush to privacy behind signs or shops on the other side, pressing together hard and fast, needing each other's breath as much as our own. Prague is for the obsessive. We are Franz and Milena, the arch under a bridge, a dancing building.

Each morning the Charles Bridge is a playground of pedestrians. It once withstood 600 years of wheeled traffic, thanks to eggs mixed in the mortar. Now there are tennis shoes and Tevas everywhere. Tourists barter for photographs of the bridge in other seasons, sit for their own portraits to be painted. Vendors sell postcards, puppets, and handmade wooden toys.

Travelers carry *Lonely Planet* and *Rough Guide*. They wear water bottles, video cameras, shopping bags.

Sometimes I'll catch a backpacker staring at the spots on my arms or legs. Alen's right eyetooth is the sharpest, leaves the deepest mark. But our clothes hide much of the proof, those stamps that say we're really here. We find the signs that point to palaces or tell us where Kafka ate, slept, and read. I wonder how it can be that my father, who loved history, never traveled these streets.

In Croatian, *sretna* is happy, *je vruce* is hot, *blizu* is near, and *gladna* is hungry. *Produzite* is continue. Alen squeezes my hand and his words waltz in my head. His eyebrows are thick, full of things I know and don't. Scholars say that languages expand and simplify upon contact with others.

Three weeks, two days. Outside a Stare Mesto building, a male street performer sings opera, the female parts. His face glows from heat, the energy of his voice. He wears denim overalls, a long strand of pearls. He is Tosca, Susanna, Aida, then Tosca again. The hotel room has become too expensive for our longer stay, so we look for a small furnished apartment.

The building manager greets us in the entryway, leads us up four flights of stairs. The residence has large open rooms, she says in English. She winks at me, explains, Like New York loft, but in Prague. We remove our shoes at the door—a Czech custom.

I squeeze Alen's hand as we enter. Below us, the singer hits notes of despair; Aida's father flees. It is the world's most tragic love story—a woman forced to chose between her lover and her father. Alen looks down at me, squeezes back.

The room is bathed with sunlight, the walls yellow, the wood floor dark with bright shadows. There is a smattering of furniture, fans, woven rugs too small for the room, an open kitchen, faucets with slow drips. An air conditioner sits near the largest window. White curtains wave from its breeze. It isn't really like a New York loft but it is amazing.

The manager walks us around the apartment twice, waves her arms at cabinets, fingers shelves. She asks if I am available to tutor her daughter in English for a slight reduction in the rent. Alen laughs, amused by our luck. I have applied for a visa extension which allows me to remain in Prague 180 days more. Alen can stay without additional papers for now, says the Czech have been good to him.

I'll leave you alone to discuss, she says, and pulls the door closed behind her. Alen and I stand in the middle of the room, touch our hands to each other's cheeks. His mouth moves in closer to mine, saying nothing but still asking. A few months, sharing this home, and then.

Well, then we do not know.

We nod. Yes.

We sign a lease when she returns, pay the deposit in korunas. She shakes our hands as she goes, says her daughter will come by to meet me. The room is hot, the days growing more humid. Alen walks around, continues to inspect. I pull my shirt over my head, use it to dab perspiration from my face. I go to the large window, press my breasts against its cold. I'd thought of doing this a hundred times on hot days in San Diego, pushing against the cool glass, looking out toward the Pacific, the horizon. Something had stopped me—a need for sanity or decorum that feels frivolous now.

The sun glares and in moments Alen is behind me, his hands running down my back, sinking into the curve of my waist. The twin towers of Tyn stand in the distance, giant cylinders wearing witches hats. Alen's hands continue down my legs, his fingers circle my anklebones.

He pushes his teeth into the back of my calf, then the flesh of my right thigh. Even with windows closed we hear the opera below. Tosca climbs the parapet; Alen pulls my skirt away.

We melt onto our knees, fuck like dogs. Alen's hands grip my waist and moments later I scream with Tosca, cry out like every grieving woman who came before me.

We lie on the green rug, watch the room change as the sun lowers. I rest my hands on his chest. Some nights he holds me so close I think my ribs must break before morning. Tonight will be like that. When my visa expires there might be Paris or Budapest or Vienna or Copenhagen. But we make no plans or promises. In our present there is no dreaming, no forever. He stares into my eyes, starts to say something, then stops himself. Our language does not allow for this part to be spoken. I answer with my lips against his, as if to say, and not to say, *Me too.*

When I was a little girl my father took me to La Jolla, to the studio of his friend, an old man, to show me an old typewriter. The man was a professor who studied Native American cultures, and his typewriter was important. He'd taken it apart, and re-carved each key to represent a character in the Chumash language. Officially, all seven dialects of Chumash had been extinct since 1965, but the professor and his colleagues at UCSD found speakers that surveyors had missed.

My father held me above the professor's desk so I could look down into the machine. Stacks of books and papers surrounded us. The room smelled like oranges and eraser shavings. The center of the typewriter was full of shadows. Isn't it great? my father asked.

Outside the studio, the coast's tallest palm trees lined the street. In strong winds, the palms that fell from those trees were the length of my father's car.

The professor put new symbols on the keys to write to his new friends, my father explained to me.

Is it magic? I wanted to know.

No, the professor said. It is emotional work.

There are no apartment numbers in Prague. Tenants hang their names on doors.

In a nearby Internet café, I find an e-mail from Rodney begging me not to live with Alen. For Christ's sake, you know so little about the guy, he wrote. *I mean, he could be a war criminal or something, couldn't he? I'm not sure I know you anymore.*

There would be no easy way to say this to Rodney: I feel safest in Alen's arms. I am myself with him—finally it makes sense to be myself. It's a sharp feeling that contrasts the old numbness. The world feels larger now and somehow I am safe in it.

In the early evenings Alen and I walk through the Open-Air Festival, lightly dazed, our bodies marked, glowing. Festival workers hand out red roses. All around us little girls put their noses against the flower petals. Alen and I touch the thorns.

A man can be so many things.

Families sit on moss-covered benches. They have come from all over Europe to mingle with singers and hear concerts outdoors. A fine *conmoción* fills the air. It is a Spanish word with no English equivalent, one my second grade teacher said with her softest voice. It is the joy held in common by a gathering of people.

The singers smile to the crowd. Their gowns are sleeveless, lined with pearls. There are more Aidas, Toscas. Tosca wears red; Aida is always in white.

In Prague you hear music everywhere, festival time or not. Walking the city is like strolling the inside of a giant music box. We spend so much time walking, arms around each other, humming into the breeze, and I think, Who needs words when there is music? When there is desire and flesh?

I look at Alen's profile, his jawline, the way he sings, then hums into an evening breeze. In Prague everything is potent, condensed. Always Alen's beauty takes me by surprise. I want this gorgeous man to keep fucking me, filling me, replacing the holes that loss left behind.

Weeks become months. As the days grow colder, there are puppets everywhere. Not the hand puppets of my childhood, but giant puppets, life-size, complex. Posters announce the arrival of performers from Prostejov. Stages appear in Old Town Square and Chotek Park. Young women in white smocks paint them green, yellow, and blue. They seem to work around the clock. We watch rehearsals from sidewalk cafes, some dark and dramatic, others delightfully absurd.

People come from all over the Czech Republic to see these giant puppets with dark eyes on bright stages. At first I think the puppets seem intensely human—vibrant expressions, baggy pants. Then I decide they are superhuman—capable of shocking, never feeling shock themselves.

When I was a teenager I kept a spoon hidden in the freezer. My first boyfriend was into hickeys. He seemed always on the verge of biting my neck and I'd anticipate teeth, even then, but they never came. The hickeys were light ones, green-blue, never deep or purple.

When I came home from our so-called library dates, I'd dig the spoon out of the frost, then cover it in toothpaste and hold it against the places on my neck. The combination of the cold and bleach would erase the hickeys before my father arrived home from his office.

How's my princess? he'd say. And I would feel terrible for a moment, thinking how the real princesses probably never hid things in freezers.

With the city's festivals and performances around us, it takes Alen and I weeks to notice that our apartment does not have a television. When we finally buy one Alen refuses to watch CNN, says foreign journalists in Croatia *were coward*. I want to know more and Alen says it is too much, that we both know more than we think.

Natalia, our landlord's youngest daughter, arrives carrying her stack of English flashcards. With red and pink markers, in her most careful writing, she makes new cards in school each week. Hello Alen, she sings, removing her shoes as he holds the door.

I pull my sweater sleeves down to my wrist, conscious of marks on my arms. Good afternoon, she calls to me as she takes a seat at the kitchen table. Her green eyes dance out in contrast to her blue school uniform. How are you? she says, playful, bursting to please. Without waiting for my answer she says, I am fine. The weather is mild. Today is Wednesday. My mother is Czech. My father is Italian. My sister likes yellow.

Natalia places her flashcards on the table one at a time, sets them up like a game. Statues/*sochy*, apricots/*merunky*, backpack/*bat'oh*, brass/*mosaz*, family/*rodina*. The cards allow her to show off the words she knows already. It surprises her teacher that her mother sees a need for tutoring. Her mother laughed when telling me this on the phone earlier, said her own favorite English word is *practice*. I offer Natalia a Sprite. She leaves her cards for a moment, holds the glass with both hands, stares at the fizzing of the liquid.

What is *awky oaky*? she wants to know. She explains that an American who sells *jizdenky* at the cinema takes customers' *korunas* then says *awky oaky*. She makes her eyes wide, nods her head as she says it.

Alen, reading on the sofa, looks over and laughs. The room is bright with afternoon sun. The sound of a neighbor's vacuum cleaner hums through the wall. It occurs to me that what the cinema man says is okey dokey.

It is an old expression, I say, no longer common. Okey dokey—they are silly words for okay, sure, or all right.

Yes, Natalia smiles, *okey dokey*. Okey dokey, she repeats.

Okey dokey, I say, and Alen joins our chorus. Okey dokey, we say, all three of us together, *okey dokey*.

Alen is a collector, loved American baseball cards as a teenager, which were nearly impossible to find in Croatia. His interest now is antique cameras. When we moved into the apartment he showed me how two of his suitcases were filled with them. With so many of the tourists gone, we scour markets on *Havelska* and *Dejvice*.

Market dealers sell amazing antique bowls and high-quality replicas of the season's performance puppets. There are robbers, chefs, and guards. Wizards, clowns, and Turks. We find old aluminum film containers, and return each evening searching for the cameras he wants.

The cameras, when we find them, are even better than I'd imagined. A French man selling old post cards and photos waves us over, points to cameras tucked away under his table. Too special to keep out, he says, made of polished woods, brass, and leather.

Alen bargains for an 1880's box camera, the signature *G. Eastman, Paris*, carved into dark wood. The one I like—called Flammang's Revolving Camera—looks like a small accordion. Alen smiles to me as I hold one camera carefully in my hands, then the other, as I peer into the lens from each side. They're beautiful, I say.

Not only relic, the French man tells me, nodding. They get picture now, if you like.

Alen buys the box camera and the French man gives him several old postcards in thanks. Present, I say, as I pay for the small accordion. Alen takes my free hand and kisses each knuckle as I say, *gift*.

Five months and two days. The left corner of the English language newspaper says LIGHT SNOW GRAINS POSSIBLE. Soon the vintage trams will stop running for the season. Marks on my body travel from my right shoulder, around my left breast, down to my navel, twist down my right leg, then up my left. These maps fade quickly now. My skin becomes even more tolerant, resistant to scars. I sit in our window, looking out to quiet gray streets. A woman pulls her purple coat tighter around her.

Alen is losing hold on his obsession with me, returning somewhere else. It is happening so slowly that he does not see. I know. You see, we are healing, losing the power of fresh pain, the superhuman push of Czech performers' red gowns, vivid new words, our eyes, mouths. He stares out this window often, not at Stare Mesto, but things beyond. When your body is your primary language, you intuit more powerfully than you could have ever imagined. My temporary scars begin to remind him of darker, deeper, and permanent ones. Until my father's death, I had always sensed when people were leaving, colleagues on the verge of departing, friends moving away. Now it seems I know again.

Once we woke in the middle of the night to sirens. I jumped from our bed and raced to the window, thinking it an ambulance, and Alen jumped after me, pulled me away from the window, thinking of bombs. We trembled together, Alen in his hell and me in my grief, until we realize it is a fire truck from the nearby station, likely called to a small kitchen fire or false alarm. We try to laugh at ourselves, but shake our heads. Only flesh, the biting, brings real expression back to our faces.

For the sake of love or something like it, Alen tries to focus on us, but something is less than it was. We feel used to each other, too familiar now to drown in the other. He would deny this and make me believe him if we had the same words. Too often his eyes just miss mine; sometimes he looks away. His mind is traveling home—to his real home, not the one we share.

Last night in the Jewish Quarter, outside Café Barock,

a Czech women tells us, first in Russian, then in English, the name of the Czech national anthem: *Where Is My Home?* Instead of appearing charmed, or looking at me with wonder, Alen looks away, shakes his head.

The fault is mine too. I have done the thing I said I wouldn't—let my mind leap into the future. I've started dreaming again. Sometimes I want to go with him, to know the real Dubrovnik, to feel his pain, even when it proves far more complex than my own. I want to hear him articulate exactly what he had intended to escape, but I am his other world.

Verb, object, subject. We've started something we cannot sustain. Biting creates a hard but temporary sensation. The linguists would call us rememberers—those who hold onto elements of a language they never fully learned.

Tonight, when his tongue lingers over me, when his teeth sink into my wrist, I'll try not to let my body say that it may be the last time. Like Aida, a princess, and Tosca, a lover, I let myself hope, if only for a moment, that I could love one man hard enough to make a world okay.

I think I must leave soon, or he will leave me, this man who filled me, who let me consume him. On the street below, people pull wool scarves tighter around their chins. The towers of Tyn seem darker against the dull sky. There are moments, walking, or tutoring Natalia and feeling his nearness in the next room, when I trick myself into thinking we can remain.

It seems true that languages cannot die natural deaths. They fade into something else, or disaster works to wipe them away. Alen believes that wars end long after their finale has been reported, and he must be right. Perhaps we are foolish to think we can measure such things at all. Battles, romances, linguistics, grief. One hundred years ago a chunk of the Charles Bridge fell into the Vltava, and still no one knows how to explain it.

In San Diego, flowers bloom year-round and I know that as a promise that no one can keep. Here the honesty of distinct seasons prevails. Tonight I'll try not to stare. Not to look at the bedside clock or say, *Here I am, so beg me to stay*. I'll try not to speak it in English, the world's killer language. I'll bite into my own arm, trying to determine how the sting I make differs from his, how it's the same.

Antique cameras now sit on every shelf in this apartment, brown and gold. We never use them—have failed to plan for future moments of looking at the past. I will not say this exactly. I will tell him that even as we fade, I crave his touch with a force I wouldn't have believed. I will explain that San Diego, when I return, will feel right only because of the maps he has made. And I'll say it lightly, because this is the thing about the Croatian language I know for sure: The last syllable of a word is never stressed.

Men's Furnishings

Tonight Jack is in the jungle. Cheryl, from her own pillow, has been able to make out sleep-slurred words like scarab, coconut, and Amazon. Cheryl hates coconuts. They have never agreed with her. When Baby finally cries, Jack uses the voice of his waking life: *Your turn.*

It's always my turn, she says.

Cheryl brings her eyes to focus as Baby bursts into her chorus in the next room. Cheryl, naked, trips over shopping bags as she nears their bedroom door. The nursery is just steps away. God fucking damnit, she says. The handle of a Bloomingdale's bag traps her ankle. Shhhh, Jack says from his pillow. They're Jack's shopping bags. He went on a spree.

God fucking damnit, she repeats. She is angry about her ankle as well as Jack's ridiculous and costly indulgences. For the past year, her only purchases have been baby things, a few maternity things on sale. Now Jack has two new designer suits, jeans, bath gels, herbal soaps, cologne, cufflinks, collar tabs, t-shirts in nine colors, three pair of track pants, a leather iPod carrying case, a Tiffany's money clip, and three silk ties he'll never wear.

When Cheryl heard him walk in earlier, heard the clacks and crinkles of shopping bags as he threw them to the rug, she was about to say, This is *so* unfair. This is the last straw. But she bit her lip because she never makes promises she can't keep. There will be future straws, she knows, bigger coconuts.

She flips the dimmer switch so the light in the nursery won't be too bright. She reaches for Baby and thinks that it is the very best thing in life to hold a baby. She had the same thought at thirteen, as a baby-sitter, but the feeling is better, nearly blinding, when the baby is your own. Jack calls from their bed, Don't swear in front of the baby.

Fuck off, Cheryl says. Fuck, fuck, fuck. Her parents swore in front of her and she came out okay. His parents never cussed in front of him, but they never kissed in front of him either.

Baby wants Cheryl's breast, of course. Baby smells like the perfect combination of powder, milk, poop, and Bounce. You are my everything, Cheryl says to her, and immediately takes it back. Cheryl was her mother's everything, and she felt smothered.

Baby eyes Cheryl as she latches on to her breast. Her eyes are so soft and true. She seems to be saying, It's okay Cheryl, we can be each other's everything for just a while longer. Baby sucks harder, and it hurts like a bitch.

Don't swear in front of the baby, Jack says again.

I only swore in my head that time, Cheryl says. Cheryl relaxes while she nurses. Her head lightens; the world slows. She hums a rhythm, watches the glow in Baby's eyes.

I'm sorry, she tells baby. I really thought he could be ready. It sounds naïve, I know. But I really thought the designer suits and spoiled brat drugs could leave his mind, and we would fill his heart. Jack has recently started a new job. He'd stayed out of work for two years. It's his own fault, Cheryl knows. It's his pattern. He has another so-called attack of the soul, quits a good job, attempts to find himself. Clearly, you're not at the mall or the gym or the beach, Cheryl told him last time. You've spent lots of time looking there already.

Baby sucks harder. Ow, Cheryl says, You're getting stronger and stronger. From the next room, Jack talks through his sleep. *Someone as educated as you should have better words.* It sounds like a lot for a man to mumble in his sleep, but he has said this sentence at least a thousand times in the last eight years. He fails to appreciate the beauty of the word fuck, Cheryl thinks.

Fuck, fuck, fuck. A versatile word. When baby grows into girl, she wants her to hold an awareness of our amazing freedom of speech amendment. She wants her to be able to tell the bad men to fuck off. Fuck, fuck, fuck, she sings. Fuck, fuck, fuck. A little mantra.

She loves the essential warmth of baby, her perfect temperature.

Every time Jack is out of work, Cheryl kicks into high gear, takes on extra assignments, pregnant or not. She is a collection consultant, an auctioneer. She has always said she'd never rely on a man to support her. Of course, the joke is on her, Cheryl realizes. She may end up supporting everyone. The so-called modern woman, Cheryl muses. She's in a funk. Not that Cheryl's complaining. Cheryl doesn't want to be a martyr, understands things could be so much worse. Women in her Lamaze class had husbands and boyfriends who made promises and disappeared. Jack's pretending is something a little different.

Oh, she wants to be more like her sister, who loves coconuts but hates men.

Men are too flawed to hate, Cheryl thinks. Sometimes the thoughts in her head annoy her. During the past year, there have been so many changes. She used to love Jack and his flaws. Now it seems she struggles to love him in spite of them. Cheryl used to indulge too, but not now, not like this.

Tonight, Baby cannot get enough. There is more love inside

Cheryl now. This pregnancy left her filled with it. She has said this to her sister, who has told her to stop romanticizing the swelling. After birthing Baby, Cheryl feared she would have to lie with ice packs between her legs forever. With Baby nursing, Cheryl remembers her own body, the normal size of her breasts. They hurt less now. She can manage the night without the white nursing bra.

So Jack has gone on a shopping spree with his first paycheck and the credit card that was supposed to be for emergencies. Never mind that Cheryl paid the birthing expenses her insurance did not cover; that she paid for everything during his time off, including his credit card bills, their condo, and their car. He must feel grateful—it would be impossible for a good person not to, and she believes good exists in him somewhere—but he rarely says so. And this is how he repays her.

Never mind that they need new towels, that people with babies don't shop for themselves. She cannot even begin to think of a way to justify his selfishness. Jack likes the idea of looking like the model dad when he takes Baby out in the stroller. We are a family, Cheryl says, not a photo shoot. Still, Jack wants to change his own name to Jax.

GHB. Those three little letters may have made him crave vials, tablets, or little white lines.

He'd called at seven from men's furnishings, high from the shopping and maybe something else. He'd been out to lunch with an old and fucked-up friend. Maybe they got wired. Maybe they bumped. See, she knew the lingo still, but just because you knew the language of a place didn't mean you had to stay there.

Maybe Jack and his friend really wanted their youth back, a couple of suited, soon-to-be wrinkled, wannabe teenagers on E. She wished her mind couldn't draw the image, oh God—Jack at a rave. He had a baby face that could go anywhere, but a rave is no place for a father.

Before Baby, this possibility of Jack's little drug indulgence would have pissed her off, but not freaked her out so much. She wasn't a total prude, after all. She wasn't living in the dark ages, she thinks, and amends the thought—there were likely some okay drugs floating around in the dark ages. She wasn't a prude, but now she was a parent.

She was a mother, and the mother, she believes, not the father, retains the rights to postpartum dementia. Jack is out of place, out of line. Even in her bad girl days she'd had it together, so what was Jack's excuse now?

Baby slept some of the evening away, so it would have been nice for Cheryl and Jack to relax together. When she said that into the phone, he laughed. Relaxing was the last thing on his mind. He'd called from Bloomies, and couldn't remember why. Cheryl had slammed the phone down, pulled a pint of Low Fat Sorbet from the freezer, and plopped down at the kitchen table with the newspaper. Always *Los Angeles Weekly* makes you feel less alone. As Jack shops miles away, she rubs pages between her fingertips, reads.

A4: Attention Wives! IF YOUR HUSBANDS ARE BETWEEN THE AGES OF 30 AND 40 and attracted to COCAINE, OPIATES, and other substances YOU MAY BE ELIGIBLE TO PARTICIPATE IN A RESEARCH STUDY. Get involved!

A9: Test your maturity level in our Awareness Workshop. 1-323-GET-HELP.

B14: *RETAIL SLUT* on Melrose. Flirt with our *SEMI-ANNUAL SALE!*

C5: Attention New Moms! The First Annual Blanket Event at THIS LITTLE BABY WEARS COTTON.

Leave the black of your workday behind. Leave that overwhelmed new dad in the car. Leave him entirely. Wear yoga pants in pastel colors. He doesn't match! Surround yourself in the smell of powder, the wonder of white and pink and yellow and blue!

She reads every ad in C and D and E and F, one through twelve. She feels too tired for articles, too muddled to consider anything about men and power. Something makes her remember the Bush-Gore election, a long time ago, a time of confused political parties and great actual parties. News of pregnant chads. Gore staffers in flux. What to expect when you're expecting.

ABCDEFG. She's hard on herself when she makes mistakes. Typos found too late on important documents—these kinds of things make her cringe. But she's not sure precisely what punctuation ruined the possibility of perfection this time, if proofreading works off the page, if proofreaders would agree she has had the right child with the wrong man.

She thinks of Tommy, a little boy from her family's neighborhood whose mother always grounded him when she found pot in the house. Everyone knew the pot was his father's—everyone but his mother. This story that used to make Cheryl laugh now only makes her cringe. She'd told it to Jack, and wonders now if he'd taken it as a warning, a dare, if he'd heard her at all.

And there's her sorbet... melted in its container.

At a barbeque last week, in the parent-filled backyard of a couple they met crib shopping at Little Folk Art, one of the moms worried about GHB, and Jack was pissed he'd never heard of it. While the young children and babies slept inside the bi-level house, teenagers kicked soccer balls and adults passed salads around a picnic table.

The mom's oldest was in ninth. GHB was the hot thing among club goers, she claimed. It would be only a matter of months before it hit the high schools, she said, and then the danger that middle school kids would catch on too.

I used to be up on these things, Jack kept saying over and over again, wrinkling his brows. He kept looking to the soccer kids, wondering how he wasn't there but here.

Wake up, Cheryl wants to say. Surprise honey! You're in your thirties! Then Cheryl made the mistake of reminding him they hadn't been to a club in five years.

Has it been that long? Jack wanted to know.

But we're up on all new things, wonderful things, Cheryl should have said.

She turned to their hosts: The German potato salad is incredible.

Jack's complexion went yellow. He put his face in his hands. The men looked away from him, shifting their eyes, awaiting breakdown. God, I really loved ecstasy, Jack said. A mom nearly dropped the seven-layer salad. Another looked like she'd been struck.

Well GHB was supposed to be easy if you could get it, the first mom said, trying to ignore Jack as she spoke. Ecstasy had been an easy score for their generation, Cheryl thought. Lightweight and easy to take. Crystal meth had been the hard one, the dark and angry one. You never wanted to find yourself in a room full of meth heads.

A clear liquid in a tiny vial. Invisible, the mom said, shaking her head. Do you know what that means? If they have it at school, they can pour it into my kid's Sprite or Mountain Dew when he gets up to go to the bathroom. They all looked at their food, but the mom wasn't going to back down. Invisible, she said again.

Cheryl moved her eyes to Jack's, gave him a discreet smile. Jack took his face out of his hands, composed his expression. It had been a long time since they had the same thought at the same time. As if, Cheryl thought. Oh yes, Jack was thinking the same thing. For this moment they're in sync. They'd been reasonably bad kids themselves, so they know bad kids never waste good drugs on straights.

Wow, Honey, make sure you try the three-bean, one of the dads said. Jack continued to compose himself. Cheryl thought,

From now on dearest, the only coke at your parties is cola, so you had better get used to this.

You're right, Jack said to Cheryl eventually. The German potato salad is killer.

Oh, how did you get so beautiful? she whispers to Baby.

She breathes in the tingly cologne smells that entered with Jack's shopping bags. Words like *compulsive* and *addict* creep into her mind. She soothes and upsets herself with the suspicion that Jack could never be so devoted to one vice that he becomes an addict. By the time Jack got home tonight with his black, silver, beige, brown, and pale blue bags, he'd lost interest in his finds. He didn't bother to hang up the track pants, unwind the ties, or unwrap the CDs.

It could be so much worse. She doesn't ever want to become a martyr.

Sure, she screamed at him. Her faced raged red even if she thought there was no way for her to win. It was the same old story. He refused any suggestion that he needed help. She could accept his behavior, or she could throw him out. She was an enabler, or she was a bitch.

Baby blinks her eyes.

In the car after the barbeque that night, filled with salad, watching Baby sleep in her car seat, her head resting in her blue neck donut, Cheryl felt suddenly full of motherly sayings that weren't so ridiculous. Things like, *You know Jack, happiness can't be purchased at $30 a tab.* Jack's fingers flew across radio buttons as he searched stations for techno. So unfair, she thought. Her baby was going to grow up, and her husband wasn't.

Sure, Cheryl wants to blame his mother, but now that she's mothering, she's much more sensitive about that sort of thing. Anyway, she has said it before. If his mother hadn't treated him like a little prince, if she had encouraged some sort of work ethic in him, he wouldn't be such a difficult brat now. And a sad, sad truth: the things that Cheryl thought cute about him pre-parenthood, at age twenty-three, were likely the things that repulsed her now.

Happiness cannot be purchased at $100 at tie. She hates E and GHB and princes and ties and all these things that don't properly accessorize the mothering of a little girl.

Jack's family lived in the past, she knows. They've spent entire holidays sitting in his parent's house talking about dead people. Attorneys, brokers, and developers in the late 1800s and early 1900s. A great-grandmother developed garden tools, a great-uncle made a fortune in detergent. The last few dollars trickled to Jack's parents. They never had a lot of money, but knew how to act. They pretended their jobs were hobbies.

Happiness is not a monogram, not a coconut crème pie.

Baby's sucking slows. Such a wondrous creature, Cheryl thinks.

Cheryl's family lived in the future. They worked like machines. They started saving for this baby—Cheryl's baby— before Cheryl was out of diapers herself. Her family was a relay team racing toward Tomorrowland, but her father died, and in their shock they kept losing the baton.

The future is no better than the past, Cheryl thinks. It's full of disappointments. You cannot ground yourself there, or plan for the unexpected. When she thinks of coconuts again, she feels a twinge of guilt for failing to value them. After all, they have milk too.

Cheryl has nearly thrown Jack out more times than she can count. She has fantasized about his state-of-the-art clothing, gasoline, and a match. Job, or no job, she will be stuck with those bills. He knows how much he can get away with, then he pushes the limits. As difficult as it would be, she doesn't fear single motherhood for a second. She realizes now something she has probably always known—he will leave the minute he freaks out completely, or the second a better deal comes along.

It's interesting—the way she loves chocolate, but can't even look at a German chocolate cake because of all the coconut. Jack always forgets about her and coconuts, comes home from the market with coconut macaroons. How easy it is for one ingredient to ruin another.

She doesn't hate the idea of being alone. But something binds her to Jack. She always thinks of that unnamed thing, remembers it through her anger. It's something like love, but even more complex. She'll remember the way he held onto her for the eighteen hours of her labor, how there he was in the moments she scrunched her face so hard she thought her head would break, felt her body stretch so far her hips might have shattered into a thousand pieces. He gripped her hand and didn't let go once, never even went to the bathroom. That memory—both of them momentarily selfless, hurting, dying with joy—brings her rushes of hope. She'll hear Jack mumble in the night, and she'll look at him in the morning, and she'll soften.

Baby keeps her eyes closed, sighs, sucks. She seems to be saying *We'll keep an eye on him together, Cheryl.* She sighs again.

You're so Zen about all of this, Cheryl says. So monk-like and wise.

Cheryl feels tingles of admiration in her own fingers and toes. It feels impossible that she and Jack were once this small and pure. She thinks that somehow, already, this child has a sense of direction. We will live in the present, Cheryl whispers. It is an important promise. Cheryl sighs with baby. She shifts her arms.

Baby gets tired. Cheryl takes her back to their bedroom and kicks aside the shopping bags, pretending they're balls. Score, Cheryl says. Baby squeaks and burps. Cheryl sits on the bed and burps her a little more. Bullfrogs, Jack mumbles from his jungle. Flying squirrels.

Cheryl isn't religious, but looks out the window and reminds the night skies how much she loves Baby. She thanks them for Jack's new job and prays, in her own little way, that he can manage to keep it. She wants him to live up to his potential. Is that so bad? She burps Baby and tells her to watch the landscape, that it is full of lessons, that the physical landscape is much like the human one. Palms, Jack says. Parrots.

Cheryl takes her hand from Baby's back for a moment, wipes moisture from her own nipple. She grabs a water bottle from the night table, takes a long drink. Nursing leaves her with the strongest thirst she has ever known. Parrots, Cheryl repeats, and names parrots' colors. Yellow and blue and red and orange and green. Do I hear one thousand coconuts? Cheryl says. Two-thousand coconuts? Three-thousand coconuts? Going, going, gone, Cheryl says. Sold! The parrot painting to the man in the ugly new clothes for three-thousand coconuts.

Oh, they've nearly depleted her savings, and she dreads the mail, all those bills, and Cheryl cannot keep living with the thought—she knows how crass this sounds—that everyone in the house is sucking off her. Baby will move to a formula, follow a plan, but not Jack.

Reptiles, Jack says. Ecuador.

Cheryl lies next to Jack with Baby in her arms. He and his jungle turn toward them as he pulls at the covers. He cannot sleep without blankets heavy around him. He is a thousand miles away and right here, beautiful and unfair. Baby closes her eyes.

Cheryl wants this specific moment to be sweet. She wants to remember it ten years from now, just this part, their physical closeness, not her disappointment. When Jack goes, and she eventually starts to love another man, and Baby is a wide-eyed girl full of questions, Cheryl wants to say there was this moment with the three of them, young with bright colors, dreams, eyes closed.

Ten Reasons Not to Sleep with a Poet

1. If he is Catholic, he will feel guilty. If he is Protestant, he will feel guilty for not feeling guilty. If he is Jewish, he will call his mother from bed.
2. He will snore, and you will not be able to get his snoring out of your head, even hours after he has left your apartment.
3. In bed, he will say things decidedly unpoetic, like, *Baby, my cock feels huge when it's inside you*, and feel rather impressed with himself.
4. He will really listen, and this deep listening will make you say things you never knew you wanted to say.
5. He might make you believe that you are really the poet. When he attempts to break up with you, his word patterns will form in your mind: *Only weeks ago, running your lips across my neck and trying to memorize the shape of my shoulder. Just weeks ago, my shoulder.*
6. You will not be able to let go of various maddening details. (a) He will speak to your hands as if they are separate

from the rest of you. (b) He will move his fingertips across your stomach, not in a sexy way, but in a way that makes you think he is comparing it to another stomach. (c) He will describe you as *delicate*.

7. He might want to make poet babies. He might cry before he makes you cry. He might have women in his past who seem a little too present.

8. Like other kinds of men, he will never understand the anguish of carrying a phone that does not ring. Unlike other kinds of men, he will seem to fall off the planet for weeks at a time, lost in a place—that goddamned place you know to be a space in his head and not an actual location.

9. Poets expect grand gestures. To your own surprise, you will deliver such gestures. You will forsake other friends and lovers, and consider wearing on a chain around your neck a small gold vial of poet blood.

10. In his car, in a rare moment where the world seems right, you will sing along with an old and overplayed Goo Goo Dolls song. You will sing, *Don't you love her like a cure?* And instead of letting you have the line your way, letting the world seem right just a moment longer, he will inform you that the line is really, *Don't you love the life you killed?*

Stalking Is a Dance

At eleven o'clock, on the last evening of the convention, dry ice is released. The Dot Banquet is going strong. Illustrators from all over the country have come to Chicago to network and drink lime punch. I notice Jonathan across the room—his dark hair, the height of his cheekbones as he laughs. He nods in my direction. We make our way through the crowd, shaking hands with other dot people, until we are in the center of things, and he's leaning into me, saying, Let's get out of here. There's a jazz club down the street.

A couple leaves ahead of us, a Professor of Dots and his former student. They dance up the stairs. He spins her. As she turns, her skirt floats into the air and she smells like air freshener. Like roses. Like Renuz-It. They stop in front of the door. The professor puts his hands on the woman's waist. They giggle and stare. Then they stare so hard the giggles stop.

Jonathan and I watch. The professor waits a moment too long before he kisses her. He should kiss her harder, I think. Jonathan nods because he knows it too. As the revolving door stops open she pulls away, says Thanks. She leaves the professor standing there. On the other side of the door, she jumps into a taxi, evaporates. He blinks his eyes, hardly believing that she's gone.

See that, Jonathan says. That's the moment that breaks a man's heart.

My friend Kari calls me at home as I pack for the convention in Chicago. She comes right out and asks me if I'll see Jonathan there. She wants to know if I'm still attracted to him, if I still believe in the ear thing. Her voice is firm. She enunciates each word: Because, she says, I've heard that he is kind of an asshole.

Perfect, I tell her. I'm grinning into the phone. I feel light and spicy, like a dill pickle. I go to my dresser, find my tomato-red thong and my diamond toe ring, and throw them into my suitcase. Kari doesn't approve; she knows I have this thing for jerks.

I work as a dot illustrator. I make pointillist portraits, like those you see in the *Wall Street Journal*. People think they're computer generated, but actually they're hand drawn, each of the millions of dots. I translate shadows of a face or a landscape in dots, onto a grid. I never use open dots. Mine are small and tight. I line them up like bricks. My ex is a Web designer. With him, things got tangled.

Jonathan is also a dot person. He illustrates books. Before I'd met him at last year's convention, I'd known his work. His form, rhythm, and use of color inspired and belittled me at the same time. A Russian woman once told me that if you nibble someone's earlobe long enough, you share in their intellect.

I tell Kari that I'm captivated by Jonathan's work. I fantasize that under the right circumstances, we could become one of the great artistic couples of all time. Like Picasso and Gilot. Nin and Miller.

Those aren't exactly model relationships, Kari points out. And you forgot Scott and Zelda, she says. Don't ever forget what happened to Zelda.

The jazz club is smoky gray. Jonathan and I take seats at the bar, marveling at the strength of the singer's voice, her long, cornrowed hair, her wondrous gold, beaded gown. She sings without breaks. She tells us of her mojo.

A bartender brings vodka martinis with fireballs floating in them. This is much better, Jonathan says. The dry ice was giving me a headache.

He keeps brushing his arm against the side of my breast. An accident, I think at first. I tell Jonathan a story about a stalker who insisted he was a choreographer; he told the judge stalking is a dance. Jonathan seems impressed that I know this.

At the bar, we kick our shoes off and touch toes. My toe ring glitters. I keep watching his profile, confirming that he has perfect earlobes. When I first notice the time, it is four in the morning.

Jonathan covers the face of my watch with his hand and says, Keep talking. I think I'm falling in love with the sound of your voice.

Fall in love with all of me, I want to say. You're drunk, I say instead.

You're not? He tilts his head. He seems alarmed, and I think I hear it—something like a car alarm sounding between his ears.

Yes, I say, I'm drunk. But not in the way he thinks.

I consider drawing him and realize my limitations. The sight of him in this club proves too extraordinary for dots. His face seems full of lines and angles. His shoulders have hard edges. It seems possible that his body defies our art. Now there's no turning back. He is becoming my dark angel, my sweet gherkin.

During a convention seminar, Jonathan displayed two works from his portfolio. At first they appeared to be the same picture, a commission for a textbook, a man and a woman during intercourse, woman on top. One is gentle, black and gray, full of shadows. The other looks bold, with yellow, orange, and fuchsia rays of light. All in dots. Thousands of dots. Do you see the difference? he asked. He pointed to the first picture. It's nighttime, and they're having sex. Then he pointed to the second. It's morning, and they're making love.

We leave the club and walk to his hotel holding hands like children. He holds my fingers tight in his until he feels sure I will not evaporate. We hum together, our mouths full of fireballs. He spins me, and I forget that this spin is not original, that it's something we saw a professor do before. The lights are out and the streets are paved with ebony. The moon is an egg. He spins me again, but I do not smell like Renuz-It. I smell like jazz. We revolve into his hotel and wait in front of the elevator for fifteen years before he kisses me just hard enough.

To get to his room from the elevator, we must find our way through an English-style garden maze. Twigs crunch under our shoes. Branches poke into our arms. Florescent lights buzz from the ceiling, and we think it amazing, that this shrubbery survives in bad, loud light. We walk swiftly at first, holding hands, then let go and start running down one path, then the next, cursing dead ends. I think that somewhere out there, beyond the maze, a hotel architect laughs at the thought of us, breathing hard, fire in our cheeks, fighting these garden halls, trapped in our desire.

The door to his room hosts a brass knob in the shape of a hand. It shines and pulls us inside. The room is dark. As my eyes adjust it becomes green. A red glow from the digital clock illuminates the nightstand and headboard. We have a brunch at the convention center in hours. He shouldn't have waited all those years to kiss me.

I should be concentrating, but I'm in awe of the artistry of the headboard. It appears to be made from a gigantic slice of cucumber, and the sight of it makes my head tingle. I know,

Jonathan says. It's amazing. But neither of us turns the light to look closer.

The truth is the furniture soothes me. Tables, ottomans, and headboards have this influence on me—the balanced grooves of them, their cold ease on a grid. Especially headboards. Then there's my adoration for cucumbers; the soft inside, the seeds. If I believed in signs, I'd say that the cucumber headboard—a furnishing of my dreams—proved me destined to be here, in this green hotel room, with this beautiful man who can draw Machu Picchu in dots.

We whisper little conversations as we undress each other. There is plenty of time for this because his pants have two hundred and twenty-nine buttons.

He says, These are some bad pants, baby.

After the first hundred buttons, my fingers go numb. My clothes have zippers, so I'm naked first. We talk about Seraut, the Inca, Miles Davis, and the Canary Islands, our bodies aching and arching the entire time.

His pants join my tomato thong and the rest of our clothes, scrambled in piles on the floor. Our chests press together, our finger tips trace the outline of each others hips, and I know I'm risking buzz kill, but I have to say this: I don't want either of us to wake in the morning and think we've made a big mistake.

He puts his nose against mine. A phone rings in the room next door—an early wake-up call for a normal person.

It would be our mistake together, he says. Then he looks down to the floor, like he's sorry he said it that way.

He's right, I think, and something startles me. He's not an asshole.

You don't seem like a real jerk, I say.

He laughs, as if he's heard it before. I move my hands to his back. He perspires from alcohol and wanting.

Hey. You seem disappointed, he says. His nose moves to my shoulder.

No, I say, but it's strange. You're not an authentic jerk, and I crave you anyway.

I nibble his left earlobe, and to my surprise, he pulls away and starts nibbling mine. It scares me that he too may want something more than sex. It delights me. I say already I adore you, and we start kissing and grabbing harder and harder, speeding things up, feeding on each other, finding our pace where it belongs.

Next to his, my brain is a weak muscle. Next to him, my mind might soar.

Like caged birds, Jonathan and I fly into each wall and eventually fall into the middle of the room. The bed catches us and my head hits the cucumber headboard and seeds land on us like rain. We reach for each other again and again with continuous, fluid motions, until I am not sure which actions are foreplay and which are afterplay, or if these terms should exist at all.

I keep getting distracted from his earlobes. There is so much more to explore. He ignores my earlobes for some time too, and focuses on my breasts. He mumbles things.

He fixates on the tattoo on my right arm, a Native American totem. He spends an eternity tracing it with his tongue, then repeating the pattern in dots on my chest, stomach and legs. And somehow, after all the sex, there is one condom left and we make love.

Sunlight darts in the window. Daisies sprout from cracks in the ceiling. Tiny gold spiders run down the walls. Purple curtains open like tulips. Fumes from chemical cleaners waft in from next door. We fall asleep, or half asleep, twisted like strings of licorice. He calls me baby. He snores rhythms into my ear.

With my ex, I had history. I had a dog, a ukulele, a townhouse, furniture, linens, flatware, stemware, paintings, magazine subscriptions, an array of unpredictable emotions, and racks full of spices. With Jonathan I have this so-called mistake, this thing we saw coming, an expression, a frolic among cucumber seeds.

I consider that Jonathan knows things about me that my ex had forgotten. He knows that I am mostly water. That I may be looking when he's not expecting it. He sees that I find my way out of mazes, that I'll put fire to my tongue. We are dot people. He knows that I can watch him forever. For three million points on a grid.

Chicago has one of the world's tallest buildings, which can be drawn in 785,921 dots. It is a city full of furniture designers. A place with stalking laws, vibrant music, and censored dance. Chicago sits on a grid, anxious and ready. Once it burned down, and built itself up again. It is a city that hides in ice every February, then trembles with elevated trains, alarms, and Spring Fever.

West of the lake and north of the river, a purple market boasts the largest cucumbers. Organic cucumbers. Hot house cucumbers. Phallic greens that travel far to land here—all the way from the coast of Spain—in this hub of jazz and blues.

Now it seems easy to imagine how the morning will go. Jonathan and I will wake at the same time, our bodies pink, bloated from attention. He will ask me if everything is okay, and I will say everything is better than okay. Then I'll wish I had said something more—something articulate and wonderful that helps to keep him in love with me. Maybe he'll curl his body around mine, sniff my hair, bite the back of my neck, and rub his feet against me.

Later, Jonathan will say good-bye from the doorway. I'll realize that I don't want to go; that this is a man to die for. In my future dreams I'll take bullets or drink poison meant for him.

Of course, I'll manage a good-bye. I'll say it in a voice I've never heard before—one that scratches more than my own.

I'll notice the deepness of his eyes, the circles around them. Jonathan will know that I'm going, but not leaving him exactly. And he will appear to me the perfect work of art, standing there in striped boxer shorts, framed by daisies and fumes.

Outside this room, past an English maze, lies a city holding seven and a half million people, most of whom never draw for a living. In front of the hotel sit thirteen taxis waiting to take people to convention centers, glass houses, malls, or somewhere they might vanish. To draw a taxi by itself, you use canary yellow dots. To depict the taxi in the world, shadowed by buildings, shined by sunlight, and in motion, you must use canary, curry, lemon, maple, mum, ginger, parchment, and mustard.

Two Girls

Both would say they like husband sex better than lover sex. Women in unhappy marriages have lovers, they think, women who are cheated become cheaters. But Tira and Paige are not unhappy or cheated. They have good sex with their husbands, but somehow they cannot get things right. They love love, and so they fuck with their luck.

They are thirty years old, not really girls at all, but since they arrived at Newport Coast that morning everyone had called them girls. Can I get you girls anything to go with your coffee? Girls, do you need parking passes? Are you the girls staying at the Forester's house?

They follow the crosswalk at Pacific Coast Highway, continue downhill through the bluffs toward Crystal Cove Beach. Skateboarders and bikers rush around them. Paige notices a wooden sign in the brush, arrow-shaped, pointing in the opposite direction toward the Shake Shack, a well-known stop on the Southern California coastline, less legendary now that it is managed by a popular restaurant chain.

The Foresters are Paige's sister and brother-in-law. Their house sits in a new development that overlooks the ocean, Crystal Cove State Park, and a well-known stretch of PCH. Paige thinks critics of the development have a point; perhaps it's overdone, too much. Years ago the hills and quiet canyons filled only with wild grass and sagebrush. Tira thinks it is breathtaking now. She says that if you ignore the English road signs as you approach from Corona del Mar, you feel like you've arrived in the Italian Riviera.

Tira has flown from San Francisco. Paige has driven from Los Angeles, an hour away and a different world. Sometimes fate gets it right. Paige's sister needed a house sitter the same week Tira and Paige wanted to get away.

Sunlight beats so hard that they squint under their sunglasses.

Paige knows Tira is used to her quiet reflections while walking. They have been friends for thirteen years. Both are recently and happily wed, a fact that surprises them somewhat. Other friends thought Tira and Paige might never marry—at least, they didn't appear to be in any rush. Tira focused on her career, liked the idea of simply dating, was markedly better at it than most of her friends. Sam caught Tira off guard, captured her imagination.

Paige hated how so many of her friends hurried into marriage or obsessed on getting there. In her head, she heard the voice of her gender studies professor reminding them that marriage was an institution that historically treated women as property. Her friends would say, Yeah, but... and she'd wonder what was supposed to come after the *but*, what it was they weren't saying.

She moved in with Brian weeks after she met him. They lived together until Brian's proposal made some degree of sense to her. They created beautiful wedding ceremonies, Tira and Sam in Rhode Island last June; Paige and Brian in Hawaii in

December. For a moment they seemed to have it all—waltzes, toasts, orchids, roses, oysters, cellos, china, and mangos.

As Tira and Paige follow Reef Point trail, embankments overgrown with purple flowers obscure the beach from their view. I think that's morning glory, Tira says. As they get closer to the sand, signs staked along the path say REVEGETATION PROJECT IN PROGRESS.

Jagged black rocks appear every few feet along the beach.

The sand is so lush, Tira says. I guess everything is rich in Newport, she laughs.

Paige points to a rock in the distance. That's my favorite one, she says. It looks like part of a giant chocolate soufflé. They're so textured because the sand level changes everyday. There aren't any breakwaters.

There's a place we can go, Tira says, near your soufflé.

They carry their beach bags to a clearing, look around, feel the ocean breeze hit their faces.

This is the life, Paige says.

She thinks how at this very moment she likes her life; how humbling that thought is. They spread their towels, overlap them. Just before the shoreline, a girl in pigtails draws a mermaid in the sand. She works fast, pulls bundles of seaweed from the water, uses it to create long hair. Paige admires her energy.

This is the life, Tira repeats.

Tira and Paige have bright careers, new homes, want babies.

They understand how lucky they've been, recognize horrors they avoided, the abuses, disorders, and addictions that have cursed too many of their peers. They've suffered losses and come out okay, so they know they should not mess things up. They feel this knowledge like a chill deep in their spine on a freezing cold night.

A woman walking past in jogging clothes says she has never seen rock formations exactly like these. Paige puts her hair in a ponytail, applies sun block to her nose. Tira sprays oil onto her arms and legs, adjusts her bikini straps.

Paige looks out on the ocean and thinks it impossible to take in this view and forget that your stay on Earth is a short one. Maybe this beach is not where she and Tira should be at all. It is so difficult to forget a lover once your feet are covered in sand.

Paige meets her lover twice a year in Tucson, Phoenix, or Sedona. She and her lover are architects specializing in resort and hotel interiors. She works in Arizona often, so her absences never seem suspect. They started three years ago, just before he married. Paige tried to hold off her guilt with all kinds of silly excuses. Pre-marriage jitters, post-marriage jitters, or maybe their timing had been off—this should have been the sort of guy she slept with in college. Sometimes fate got it wrong.

In the first hours of their weekends together, she'd concentrate hard to hear his words, because she'd feel so distracted watching his lips. Sometimes she put her fingers on them, traced their movement. She wanted to feel everything he said. And he didn't find that freaky, just incredibly sexy.

At the end of the weekend, she would kiss him goodbye and mean goodbye. He hadn't set out to be a shit to his fiancé, so the guilt got to them both. But months later his email would appear, and she'd agree to a plan. The thing that surprises her most: she feels like she has known him forever.

Tira sees her lover twice a month in Washington. She handles government relations for Pacific Rim financial groups. He serves as legal council for one of her clients. Each time he greets her at Dulles Airport—Tira hates car services, likes to be met in person—she tells him this time is the last time. He tells her she keeps mistaking the beginning for the end. She's used to being right, doesn't like to be corrected.

He holds her doors, carries her bags, insists on paying and

driving—lovely gestures on their own, but together, her best friend Paige might them find suspect. This isn't the antebellum South, she would say. Tira can think of a hundred reasons why her lover would be wrong for her even if she weren't married. It impresses her—feeling this pull to a man who doesn't know her at all. Like Paige, she can't seem to give up her adventure.

Tira and her lover attend the same meetings after they've been together, pretend for their colleagues they haven't been face to face for some time. Every time she sees him alone, the first thing out of her mouth is, What am I doing? I just got married.

He says, I don't know what you're doing, but please don't stop.

Yet Tira and Paige have planned these days off in Newport as a sort of rehab, saying they want to stop, even if it turns out they do not possess what it takes. I've got to end it, Tira keeps saying. It's all wrong. There's too much at risk.

They notice sailboats near the horizon line. Tira says, It's beautiful here. I can't wait for Sam to see it. I know, Paige says. Brian wants to move down here when we're older.

Brian, now working as a packaging designer, is attending a conference in Sacramento this week. Sam, a baseball player, has spring training in Miami. And the lovers—those other men—spend the week exactly where they should, at their respective homes with their respective wives. So the girls lie on the beach alone, together, dwelling.

Tira puts down her book, grabs the tanning oil to reapply. Sunbathing is another thing they keep promising and failing to give up.

Paige wraps her t-shirt around her camera bag. When they walk the beach later she wants to photograph the Cove's 1920s ramshackle cottages. Developers and conservationists continue to fight over them. She plans to get them on film before they're taken over. At this moment she feels too tired, cranky, as if she woke too early. She feels frustrated with herself. People with secrets to keep should at least be morning people, she thinks.

Several seagulls poke along the shoreline. One squawks at another.

Do you really think it's true? Tira rubs oil onto her legs.

What? Paige says.

That you'll never be with him again.

I'm not sure, Paige says. She admits she may lack the strength to say no. More than that, she fears—no, she *knows*—he'll never ask again. She hates herself for wanting him to.

A group of girls set up towels several feet away. They're all blonde, freakishly tall, wearing UC Irvine tanks over athletic style swimsuits.

I can't even imagine it, Tira says, watching them. College without snow.

I know, Paige says. Everything still seems so different here.

Tira grew up in New York, Paige in New Haven. They met at Brown, graduated and landed West Coast jobs.

Do you remember, Paige says, the vulgar things everyone used to say in college—all those smart kids sounding so stupid about sex? Like when a girl was sleeping with guy, but not really going out with him, everyone would call him her *schlong pie*.

Tira imitates a breezy college girl voice: Hey Collette, how's your schlong pie?

Paige laughs, adjusts her sunglasses. That's great, she says. Of course, it would have been funnier if one of Collette's schlong pies wasn't my boyfriend.

Yes, Tira says. But now he's fat and bald and living in New Jersey.

Paige's face softens. I promised myself then that I'd never be with another woman's man.

The wind picks up, blows sand onto their towels.

Well who knew? Tira says. Back then who knew anything at all?

One of the tall blondes runs over, asks to borrow Paige's sun block for her nose. Paige thinks the blonde looks too young to be a college student, and the thought makes her feel old. As the blonde rubs her nose, she notices Paige's camera.

I brought mine too, she says. What are you shooting?

The cottages, Paige says. And you?

I brought it in case the dolphins show up. The water is so warm and gentle here that dolphins come to have their babies.

Tira turns away, flips to her stomach as she hears the word babies.

Thanks, the girl says, and strides over to rejoin her friends.

It's hot, Tira says. She removes her sunglasses and closes her eyes.

Paige recalls how Brian joked with her one morning that she'd never notice another man. How do you know? Paige teased, watching him from their bed.

Brian posed in front of the mirror, used his fingers to fix his hair.

Because, he said, I am the hottest thing since sliced bread. Just look at me. You'd have to be insane to look at anyone else.

On the brown beach, in the afternoon sun, Tira closes her eyes, smiles softly, mumbles through dreams. Paige cannot get comfortable. She half-sleeps and remembers.

Paige. At a Phoenix resort, ten weeks earlier, there was a moment, when he was on top of her, when their sex must have felt too much like something more. He stopped, moved his hands from her hips, stared into her eyes, said, I think we have to be clear on what we're doing here. I think we have to agree that we're fucking and not making love.

Fine, Paige said to him. So fuck me.

The rest of the night they fucked like rock stars. They did it on top of the table, desk, dresser, in every chair, against the closet doors, and so hard into the bed that the headboard punched divots into the wall. Six condoms and several more than six orgasms later, they felt too wound up to sleep. He opened champagne from the minibar. The wire hood around the cork cut his hand open and she ran to the bathroom, grabbed a towel. He tried to stop her from wrapping it around his hand, told her blood would stain.

You want to be responsible now, she laughed. We've upended a desk and ruined a wall. I don't think anyone will worry too much about a towel.

She called Tira the next morning. You're not going to believe this, she said.

I have goose bumps, Tira said. Tell me.

They're pregnant.

Oh my God, she said. How did he tell you?

He didn't have to, Paige said. At dinner I just knew. Something's different, I said. And he said, I really feel like an ass now. My wife is… we're expecting.

So how did you leave it? Tira asked.

Paige told Tira once that the present risks felt awful, but a man with a family—how could she even look at herself? It would be too much.

It's over, Paige said. This is it.

Oh God, Tira said. So a sad-song sort of goodbye?

Clearly Tira was the romantic.

Actually, Paige said, it was more like Def Leppard's farewell tour.

Three days later, Tira called Paige, back in Los Angeles. You're not fucking going to believe this one, she said. Our synchronicity is ridiculous. Mine is expecting too.

Tira. In Washington, they had exchanged smiles, stolen so many knowing looks among their business associates that there seemed no need to pretend. She wasn't sure how, but in a room full of suited men, she always knew where he stood. If spotting him had been a game, she would have won each time.

She accepted his invitation to Capital Grille, and standing in the bar, before the host showed them to their table, his lips pressed into hers and she couldn't believe it. There she stood, in public, meeting his challenge, pouring everything she had into that kiss.

Anyone they knew on Capitol Hill could have walked in and seen them. If they realized it, they didn't care. A stock ticker over the bar told patrons of values rising and falling. Congressional types ordered sashimi appetizers—raw meat feeding raw power. Only the kiss mattered. In those minutes everything else drifted away.

Paige. In Tucson, a year ago, he stopped her as they walked from a hotel ballroom, put his hands on her face, said, I'm not in love with you. I know it must seem like I am, but I'm not.

And something stirred inside her, kept her from taking the moment too seriously.

She smiled and he looked relieved. Then she laughed. Yeah, right, she said.

She knew what this was. He wanted the upper hand, and she wouldn't give it to him. Then he kissed her, or maybe she kissed him, but however it started she knew in that moment she stood exactly where she meant to, that if he stopped kissing her a second too soon, she'd stop breathing entirely.

Tira. They decided to get away from the Hill, meet at a little inn in Virginia. Tira's meeting ended early, so she left the city hours ahead of him, drove to Alexandria.

She loved Old Town, the cobblestone blocks of Prince Street, historic markers at every corner. She passed the Torpedo

Factory—a mall in the very place WWI torpedo parts had been made—where she saw tourists shopping, only a few boats in the marina.

She drove around, parked her rental car and walked to Gentry Row, made calls to her San Francisco office as she strolled. Then she saw them, sitting on a blue silk pillow in the window of a new shop near the Athenaeum—a pair of vintage Hermès cufflinks, the perfect gift.

When he arrived at the inn, the wrapped box sat waiting at the bedside table.

I love gifts, he told her, but I'm not used to being the recipient.

Open, she said, smiling.

When he saw the cufflinks, the solid, simple elegance of them, he told Tira they were incredible, that no one had ever given him anything like them.

In that moment, he appeared so soft, so touched, that Tira pressed her body against his, held her arms around him, rubbed her hands along his neck.

He's more romantic than I am, Tira told Paige later.

That's scary, Paige said.

Paige. She hasn't heard from him since the quiet, rainy morning after Def Leppard's farewell tour. He said he felt glad that they had been friends first, that they had something to go back to. She wanted to call Brian then, to hear his voice. She wanted time to stand still just a little longer, while this gorgeous, naked man dressed. She slid into a robe, scanned the room for her umbrella.

His flight was early, so he'd leave before her, a symbolism not lost on Paige. She would have predicted that she and Brian would be pregnant first, that she'd have news to initiate the end. She laughed at herself. She realized, staring at her lover's bare ass as he stepped into boxer shorts, that she felt behind, no pun intended.

What's so funny? he said.

Nothing, she said. Sometimes I feel like we're characters in a movie.

She noticed her umbrella then, on the desk behind her briefcase. It was her favorite, small and black, a silver handle. She'd made a reasonable effort not to lose it.

The thing about movies, he said, buttoning his shirt, is they come to an end.

She grabbed her umbrella then, aimed and threw it across the room. You're going to need this, she said.

Tira. In Washington, in the first month, he told her he truly, madly, loved her, that all she had to do was say the word and he'd leave his wife.

They sat in her room at Hotel George eating room service hamburgers. Tira had wanted to go out, but feared they'd run into someone who knew them.

She reminded him that she had a husband, she'd made vows.

He grew annoyed with her and didn't stay that night. Tira called Paige.

Is this irony? she said. People overuse the word so much that I no longer remember what it means.

Do you love him? Paige asked.

He told me I was the one he'd been waiting for. I guess I showed up a little too late.

Paige didn't change the subject.

I love him, Tira said, but he is not the love of my life. I told him that.

And? Paige said.

He said that I'm wrong, that I should mark his words,

we'll be together some day. And I just stared at him. He seemed stressed and bewildered. He meant it.

Tira sighed. It's crazy, she said, it could never work. For one thing, how would we ever trust each other?

There's your irony, Paige said.

The breeze sprinkles sand onto their feet and legs as they walk toward the collage of cottages. They have pulled hiking shorts over their bikinis.

It's amazing how people built these, Tira says, but didn't own the land under them.

There must have been a feeling that people cannot really own this, Paige thought. She looked around at the brown beach, the winding planks leading to the brush-filled bluff, the bluest patch of sky, still, somehow, smog-free. Technically someone did own the land. A rancher owned the entire county. It amazes Paige every time she's here—that so much can belong to one person.

The landowner didn't seem to mind the squatters or their cottages. If his private pocket of beach wasn't inviting enough to them, the pile of wood at the shoreline was. A lumber ship capsized in the 1920s so all the building materials they needed collected right here. For the first few summers, families returned to the Cove with their tents and camping gear, believing their cottage would have been discovered and torn down during the winter. Some of these same families lived here for three generations before the state made them leave.

Paige steps off the planks and onto a path in the brush. Let's walk to the top of the bluff first, she says. I'll photograph them from above, then we'll move in closer.

Tira pulls her phone from one of the pockets in her shorts. I felt it vibrate, she says, but it must have gone straight to voicemail.

Your office? Paige says.

Not exactly. She waits a few beats before she confesses: He and I talk on the phone a few times a day.

Risky, Paige says, but she knows Tira knows this.

Yes, Tira says. I keep telling him that, but we don't have your restraint.

Paige and her lover have rarely spoken on the phone. They'd worked hard to keep their time together separate from the rest of their lives. Too hard, she thinks now. They'd followed little rules and broken big vows. Two weekends, six emails—two each for planning purposes, one each to say how amazing it was—and all other contact business-related. In trying to be careful they'd been practical and cold.

Aren't you worried Sam will use your phone and see the call log?

I thought of that, Tira says. So I programmed his number as Yamada Kayse Corporation, one of my new clients.

God, you're good at this, Paige says.

I know, Tira says, and her voice cracks. Her eyes go wide, like she might cry.

From the top of the bluff, the cottages look lost, scattered. In the other direction, they see the coast highway, cars sliding along at a speed that feels out-of-sync with the Cove. Tira tucks her phone carefully in her pocket. Paige turns back to the cottages, notices an abandoned rooftop garden, a corner where someone has painted a white peace sign, a Ban the Bomb.

We're such cowardly cheaters, Paige says. We never even say their real names aloud.

Tira says, It's hot here. And please don't say cheating. That word makes me sick to my stomach.

Okay, Paige says. Our bad behavior.

Better, Tira agrees. Cheating is such an ugly word. It makes us sound like narcissist assholes. Or politicians.

They continue toward the aqua cottage.

I still hate it, Tira says, the way people are always telling me how lucky I am that Sam is a confident man, that he'd never feel emasculated by my career. Blah, blah, blah.

Sam is a professional athlete, but not the sort who receives obscene salaries or large endorsement offers. He bounces back and forth between the major and minor leagues, leaving Tira unsure whether attitude or skill keeps him tied to the cusp.

Brian makes constant job changes, complains that he never feels fulfilled, and has spent his working-life at entry level.

Paige shakes her head. If Brian and Sam earned more money than us, no one would champion us for being cool about it.

Paige positions her camera, zooms in on one of the boards that makes up the porch. Tira looks amused. It's marine board, Paige explains. She snaps the photo, looks to the screen around the porch. Original parts of some of the cottages were made from old boats. Porches were enclosed later. People added rooms or wings as they needed them.

Paige and Tira have discussed before that they're fooling around with men who know their careers, understand their ambitions. There's more to it, Paige thinks, something she's only on the verge of understanding.

I'm annoyed by the idea that we're acting like spoiled middle-aged men.

Actually, Paige sighs, I think we're all woman.

They walk toward the brown shingle cottage. I'm not sure I appreciate these enough, Tira says. I'm not sure I'm seeing what you're seeing.

Paige climbs to a tall rock, puts her hand on Tira's shoulder for balance. That's the way I feel when I look at an Excel spread sheet, Paige laughs. She positions her camera toward the roof to photograph the gable. Designers tend to disregard vernacular architecture, Paige says, but I think it's full of lessons.

Tira holds Paige's camera as she jumps from the rock.

Tira looks to the horizon, her thoughts far away. Maybe it's the French in you, she says.

Maybe, Paige laughs, but I think our selfishness is undeniably American.

They turn to face the hillside cottage.

So the cottages nearest the water are blue, Tira says, but these are brown, sort of blending with the bluff.

Exactly, Paige says. Frank Lloyd Wright would approve.

See, I'm catching on.

There's hope for you yet, Paige laughs.

They gaze at a hillside cottage, one that kept its original layout. The windows came from old train cars, the door handles from an estate sale in Hollywood. Paige snaps pictures.

The psychology of cheating... Paige says.

She adjusts her camera. Tira glares.

Bad behavior, I meant to say.

I don't know if I want to hear this, Tira says. Can we stay on architecture?

Well, if we believe nothing is lacking in our relationships with our husbands, Paige says, and we're filling a void, we have to consider what that might be.

Our mothers, Tira says.

They follow the planks toward the next grouping of cottages. The sky around them looks impossibly blue. Paige and Tira lost their mothers when they were young. Neither mom lived to see her fortieth birthday. Tira was only a toddler when her mother went into the hospital for the last time. This grief is the first thing they understood about the other, the thing that keeps them separate from others.

They peer in the windows of several cottages, notice sloping floors, tilted walls.

I can imagine Cove summers, Tira says. Luau parties at night, fresh strawberries in the morning, cool drinks on their porches at sunset.

Paige points to the largest cottage. There are patios opposite each other and two outdoor showers. Cove legend says two brothers built that one, then divided it down the middle in the 1940's after they'd had a fight.

They fought over a woman, Tira guesses, and wanted to forget they had ever shared anything. Paige leads them toward a two-story cottage, walks around it to find the best angle for her photo.

Even if it's over, Tira says, you'll have nice memories.

Memories, friendship, consolation prizes. Actually, Paige admits, I think the *we'll always be friends* thing is a bunch of crap.

I wouldn't be so sure, Tira says. She pushes her hair behind her ears.

Tira was always better at those transitions, Paige thinks now, friend to lover; lover to friend. Tira's ex-boyfriends attended her wedding.

Seriously, *let's be friends* has always seemed like such a line to me, Paige says. Like, you have soft skin, you have beautiful eyes. I'm blessed by some incredible friendships. And when I look at those other friends, I am not stuck with the memory of my tongue touching their testicles.

Tira shakes her head. But you do have soft skin, she says, and beautiful eyes. And maybe you can forget about the testicles someday.

You know we should both be back in therapy, right? Paige says.

The last time I was back in therapy... Tira says.

Seagulls fly above them. Paige remembers. The last time Tira went to a therapist he fell asleep ten minutes into the session, started snoring and drooling.

Paige points to a small, brown shingle cottage. That one has a secret room under the porch, she says.

Tira says, Do you ever think you're in this situation because there's so much love inside of you? That you have more love to give than one man can possibly receive?

Tira is the kind of friend who will always let her friends off the hook.

Paige smiles, puts the camera around her neck, holds Tira's hand. I've been thinking that same thing about you.

They continue toward an L-shaped cottage, the only one painted yellow.

We never said it, Tira says.

What?

Tira laughs. Forsaking all others. We wrote our own vows, with no forsaking.

So we're free on a technicality, Paige says. Although I think infidelity is against the law in most states, isn't it?

Not ours, Tira says. And please don't say infidelity. To tell you the truth, I'm so annoyed he was sleeping with his wife.

Paige shakes her head. You're serious?

Totally.

But you've been sleeping with your husband, Paige points out.

That's different, Tira says. She pauses. I was sleeping with my husband, saying unequivocally that I love my husband, that I have no intention of leaving him. But he was sleeping with his wife, telling me that he loved me, that he was willing to leave her.

You actually have a point, Paige says, nodding.

A good one, Tira says.

Paige snaps the yellow cottage. Just one more, she says, over there, by itself.

They look to the largest one, the famous one, Cottage Thirteen, where the movie *Beaches* was filmed. They follow the handmade boardwalk, notice its sash windows and outhouse. They look at the deck, overgrown with weeds.

It was such a beautiful movie, Tira says.

Paige nods, turns toward the ocean. Sometimes I wake from a dream, she says, and I don't know what the dream was, but I've just said I love you. The words are practically still on my tongue. And I have no idea if I said it to Brian, my mother, or him.

That's so sad, Tira says.

Paige turns back to the cottage and snaps photos of its white picket fence until she finishes the roll of film.

It doesn't look abandoned exactly, Tira says. It looks like you could go inside and take a nap.

Back on the sand they remove their shorts and return to their towels near the soufflé. They rest on their elbows, watch sunlight create sparkles along the surf, pass a bottle of water back and forth.

Lifeguards cruise around the beach in a red SUV. They shift gears, spray sand from their tires, wave to Cove regulars. The freakishly tall girls play Wiffle Ball. The number of sailboats in Paige's vision multiplies. The waves seem to come in faster. She loves the sound of the ocean, the sound of movement.

So I have a variation on the mother theory, Tira says. She stares at Paige with wide eyes, takes a deep breath.

Paige adjusts her towel, turns to face her.

The thing I fear most is that we'll share our mother's fate. She lowers her voice. Maybe we're leading double lives because we're so fucking afraid that we're only allowed half a life. Paige stares at Tira, and although she has thought of this a hundred times before, she feels her eyes water, has no idea what to say.

They climb sandy wooden stairs built into the bluff, back toward Reef Point, stopping to read a placards about shore birds. They cross the bike path and PCH, follow the sidewalk until they are in front of Trader Joe's. Orange cones and ribbons mark off the parking area. Three boys in surf shorts secure a metal platform onto large blocks, a temporary stage. Another sits Indian-style on the cement nearby, picking at his guitar, singing, *I kissed you at the Bay Bridge; I've kissed you on Bourbon Street.*

I love songs about kissing, Paige says.

One of the platform boys hears her, says something to his friends, who stop what they're doing, smile. Are you girls coming for the party?

They appear to be sixteen or seventeen, tanned and cocky, equal parts confident and unsure. What party? Tira says, smiling, flirting back. Paige loves the way she's disregarding that she has fourteen years on them at least.

Trader Joe's is hosting a block party tonight. Our friend here is playing.

The guitar boy looks up from his kiss song, nods in their direction. A California boy who apparently doesn't wear sunglasses, his bangs hang over his eyes.

Maybe, Tira says, remembering to shrug her shoulders in a vacant, sixteen-year-old way.

They continue toward Starbucks. God, Paige says. Block parties belong to market chains now? When did that happen?

Tira laughs. The good thing to remember—we're still getting invited.

It's off-balance, the way parties were better then, and sex is better now.

Tira nods toward the Starbucks line, out the door and into the courtyard. They decide they don't need lattes, continue up the hill to Paige's sister's house.

At dinner tonight, Tira says, we need a nice Chardonnay and a game of P.Y.O.

Paige laughs. You're right, that's exactly what we need.

P.Y.O is a game their housemates in college invented. Petty Yourself Out. When it's time for a boyfriend to go, you name every unattractive detail about him you can muster. Petty details are encouraged, earn bonus points. You attempt to petty yourself out of lust. It never works, of course, but you feel better anyway. Paige added her own discretionary rule—that you play with only one other participant, one you trust not to repeat anything said in the game. It was incredible, Paige remembered, how cruel the housemates could be.

They drop their things in the foyer. I did some P.Y.O on my own the other night, Tira confesses. They spread their arms and spend a minute standing in the crisp breeze of the air conditioning. Conveniently enough, she says, his wife has a cat.

Paige breathes in the smell of the beach coming from their skin. Both she and Tira have burns on their shoulders. One of the many things they have in common is an intense dislike for cats—those beady eyes, the way they hide and creep around.

Ugh, Paige says.

So to keep myself from calling his mobile, I imagined him at home, in a horrible pair of coke bottle glasses—he always wears contacts with me—lying on a sofa, reading a brief, as the mangy, filthy cat jumps onto his chest, smelling all tuna and kitty litter, then curls up and stays there. I was never so unattracted to him.

That's the worst image you can come up with? Paige says.

Oh no, Tira says, there's more.

They go to the kitchen, grab Diet Cokes from the fridge, lean against the granite island. Tira says how Sam would love this kitchen, the vegetable sink, the double oven, a six-burner stove.

Mine waxed his back for me, Paige laughs. I didn't mind his back hair; it just occurred to him that this is what men having affairs must do.

That's fair, Tira says. I'm guessing you removed some hair for him too.

The worst bikini wax pain of my life, Paige laughs.

Ouch, Tira says. You need to give that up and get laser.

When I left the day spa an old woman who had been in the

massage room stopped me in the parking lot. She said, Honey, I could hear your scream two doors down. Next time you need to remember to drink a few shots of Jack Daniel's first.

That's wise advice, Tira says.

I know, Paige laughs, we probably could have learned a lot from her.

Paige likes her sister's home, the soft colors and modern comfort of it, but feels now it's too present tense. The living room furnishings brand new, the photos on the mantle all recent. Nothing suggests a life before this room.

Tira and Paige have showered, changed into jeans and knit tops. Tira sits on the sofa with her laptop, checking e-mail. Paige adjusts the window shades to reduce the glare on Tira's monitor.

What is the coolest thing he ever said to you? Tira asks.

Well, Paige hesitates. It's not sweet or romantic, but maybe it's cool.

Tell me, Tira says.

Paige sits next to Tira on the sofa, leans back, stares at the vaulted ceiling.

He said that I have starred in every masturbatory fantasy he has had in the past three years.

Oh my God, definitely that qualifies as cool, Tira says.

Paige looks out the window to the ocean, calm from this vantage point, a sea of blankets.

They shop before dinner. In only one hour at Fashion Island, Tira purchases sling-back shoes, a skirt, and two sports bras. Paige finds a lingerie set, a computer bag, and lipstick.

It's official, Paige says, as they linger at Fireside Cellars, in the aisle of featured wines. I have no will power, not a trace.

Tira pulls all of her shopping bags into her left hand,

reaches for a bottle of Kistler Chardonnay with her right. I think that's entirely possible, she says.

A realty sign in the parking lot advertises a new development of townhouses, PERFECT FOR YOUNG PROFESSIONAL COUPLES, each featuring a three-car garage. When did all this begin? Paige wonders. When did we all start wanting so much more than we need?

In the car, Tira checks her phone, finds two text messages. *Call me*, from Sam, and *I miss you*, from her lover. Paige adjusts her seat again. Always she's concerned that she sits too close to the wheel when she drives.

Tira says, Do you remember when you first told me about him?

Paige nods. They'd gone to a wine tasting event for Brown alums in San Francisco. They'd been talking about their mothers that day and the room seemed too small, the air too thin, and the wine wasn't going down fast enough.

Paige told Tira that the first time she slept with him, she felt completely understood.

You told me that in case anything ever happened to you, you wanted me to know that you had that feeling, that moment.

I really said that? Paige says. She looks into the rear-view mirror.

Yes, Tira says.

Paige looks at Tira, next to her in the car, dusk setting around them. She knows that Tira is deciding. Tira wants to determine how she'll manage her life and love when this week ends, if she's capable of reaching for domesticity over drama, craving the routine over the reckless. For Paige, there is nothing to decide, the affair set up to be temporary, the end always looming. Paige is grieving.

Paige presses the scan button on the radio over and over again. A bumper sticker on the red van in front of them says GIVE WAR A CHANCE.

It's hard to find, isn't it? Tira says.

What? Paige says, reducing her speed, giving up on the radio.

Def Leppard, she says. They don't get the airplay they deserve.

They laugh, but Paige feels her mood shift back faster than the gears.

As they turn onto Avocado Boulevard, Paige says, I think I need to revise my earlier answer. The coolest thing he ever said to me was that he likes his life, and he knows I like mine. I'm not sure how he said it exactly. I was distracted by his lips.

Tira reaches back to grab their jackets from the rear seat. Evening temperatures drop quickly in Newport. Maybe he was just babbling then, Tira says. Blah, blah, blah. Can we please stick with the other answer?

They're late for dinner by Newport standards, so the crowd at Gulfstream begins to thin. They wait only a few minutes for a table. She smells him before he speaks—a whiskery drunk turns from the bar to tell Paige she has beautiful eyes. Tira laughs. See? she says.

The host leads them through the darkened room, past photos of giant swordfish, past leather-lined booths, to a candlelit table by the window.

Could we use another word for them? Tira says, as they scan the menu. Lover is starting to bother me.

Paige laughs. This is very Washington of you, she says, this euphemistic speech. 'Bad behavior' is to 'cheating' like 'friendly fire' to 'we shot our own guys.'

What is this, Tira laughs, the S.A.T.?

They notice one of the girls from the beach three tables away. They can't see the man she's with, but notice she's twirling her hair in her fingers, rolling her eyes, bored.

Do you worry that it's more than *want*?

Want can prove pretty powerful, Paige says.

So what if you love him more than his wife does? What if he *needs* you?

He clearly doesn't, Paige says. That's what makes it so confusing. We come to each other well loved.

I would die for either of them, for him or for Sam.

Paige nods, stares at the votive in the middle of the table. Tira has always trusted Paige's advice, yet Paige feels unqualified to give it now, even as Tira's best friend, even as a fellow adulterer. Tira and her lover spent long evenings together, talking, crying, before they ever had sex. Tira's is an emotional affair that became sexual; Paige's was the other way around.

At Brown, they had been the silly sort of girls who clung to their virginity like life vests. When they finally *lost it*—a phrase Paige detested because she knew loss and it felt nothing like that—Paige, nineteen, felt angry that she'd waited so long, that she'd denied herself those potentially beautiful connections. Tira, at twenty, felt minor regard for the actual sex, but craved the attention that followed and preceded it.

A man wearing a fish-shaped tie leaves bread at their table so quietly that Paige barely notices him. Tira studies the menu.

Sex with Brian is beautiful. The way Paige loves him seems instinctual now, like she has come to know his body as well as her own. Sex with her lover is curious, nervous, frantic. Everything accelerates, a fog moves over them. She feels drunk with him, urgent and disoriented, like she has lingered too long in someone else's dream.

The waiter looks relieved when she approaches them. Finally, a good table. I've had lots of crazies tonight, she explains. Paige orders scallops; Tira chooses sea bass. The waiter recommends the new house wine, a Sauvignon Blanc. She thanks them, says everyone before them tonight was so high maintenance.

It's sort of funny, Paige says, that she assumes we're low maintenance and sane.

Tira tucks her handbag further under the table, grabs her napkin from her lap before it slips to the floor. P.Y.O., let's go, she says. You first.

Paige hesitates. I'm not sure my brain is numb enough yet for this petty game.

The wine is on the way. Go as petty as you can, Tira reminds her.

Okay, Paige says. She holds the stem of her water glass.

First complaint, he wears his pants far too baggy. They're always big, heavy, pleated things that make him walk like a little old man. Cute, but what's wrong with a pair of jeans?

Well he doesn't sound that sexy now, Tira admits.

Exactly, Paige says. And why should his wife and I be the only people in the world who know he has a great ass?

Tira laughs. The candlelight makes her blush sparkle. Mine has a lame tattoo, she says. I love tattoos, Paige says. She had wanted Brian and her to get tattoos together before their wedding. Brian had refused.

Not this one, Tira says. It's the Texas A&M logo. It's across his right upper arm, a huge red T in the middle.

You're kidding... Texas?

I'm not. It gets worse. He's from Houston—she takes her voice to a whisper—and he's a Republican.

No way, Paige says.

Tira rolls her eyes, nods. It's true. She grabs her glass. I'm from a long line of devoted Democrats. Hell, I interned for Senator Kerry, and now I'm fucking a Republican.

To be fair, Senator Kerry married a Republican, Paige says. But yes, worlds worse than baggy pants, Paige admits. You win this round.

So I go first this time, Tira says. Here it is: He parts his hair like Brian Williams.

Paige laughs. Well, I like Brian Williams.

Fish Tie Guy fills their wine glasses. He smiles not exactly at Tira, but her glow.

Yes, but I'm sure even Brian Williams didn't have that wide part at twenty-something.

Back up, Paige says. She leans in, bows her head. He's in his twenties?

Yes, I thought I told you. Tira pushes her hair behind her ears.

Wow, Paige says, sitting back, a little stunned. He's a Young Republican.

It's not a big deal, she says. He's extremely accomplished for his age. He's like twenty-six going on sixty.

Tira avoids Paige's eyes and continues. The part itself is so wide... She draws an imaginary line on her head with her forefinger.

Hold on, Paige says. I'm still digesting the age thing.

She almost wants to joke about baby powder, but the baby thing isn't particularly funny in the present context of things.

What's a few years? Tira says, shrugs her shoulders.

All this time Paige had imagined Tira's lover older. She has to revise his image in her mind's eye. Her own lover is the same age she is, the same height, sign, and profession. She worries for a moment that she has fucked the male version of herself, that maybe it's all masturbatory.

The part reminds me of the Little People toys I had when I was five, Tira says.

Oh my God, Paige laughs, you mean he has the Fisher Price hair part. She remembers those toys too; boy mini-dolls that came with boats, farms, or parking ramps.

Yes, Tira says. That's funny, that's it exactly.

Paige takes a slow drink from her glass.

Okay, she says. Remember when I said he had a perfectly shaped penis?

This is going to be good, Tira says, go on.

I'm reconsidering that, Paige says. Without getting into too much detail, well... the rim is really thick.

Ouch, Tira says, and grabs for her water. I think that's a tie.

Okay, Paige says. You go first.

This one is so petty, Tira says.

The name of the game, Paige laughs.

So the middle of his nose is longer than the outer sections. When I look at his profile, I see the inside of his nostril.

Wait, Paige says, you're saying his septum dangles?

Yes, Tira says, I think so.

But that's not terribly uncommon. In fact, it's really normal.

I know, Tira says, my tick. But it is terribly annoying, noticing yourself looking inside a man's nostril all the time.

Paige laughs, shakes her head. Fish Tie Guy returns, adds a new votive to the center of their table.

You can't beat that one, can you? Tira says. She tears at a piece of bread.

In only three words, Paige says. She waits, lets Fish Tie Guy move out of earshot.

Let's hear it.

Dorky climax smile, Paige enunciates.

Now that's hilarious, Tira says. But the more I think about it, it's adorable too. Are you serious?

I'm afraid I am, Paige says.

The waiter appears with their entrees.

Then that wins for sure.

As Fish Tie Guy takes the empty wine bottle, the girl from the beach glides past their table toward the bar. She wears a short skirt and heels four inches high at least. Kinky hair lingers down her back. She looked freakishly tall on the beach; now she seems Amazonian.

When Tira and Paige finally leave their table they notice her at the bar without her date, speaking into her cell phone. The rescue call, Tira says. She wants one of her girls to help save her evening.

Paige nods. As coeds, she and Tira made those calls too.

The creepy drunk leers at Amazon Girl, moves to the seat next to her.

Big mistake, Tira says.

Are those fuck me pumps? the drunk says, slobbering, loud, pointing to the shoes.

Amazon girl removes her phone from her ear, holds it like a weapon. They're Chanel, she says, sneering. I'm pretty sure that makes them *fuck you* pumps.

Impressed, Tira and Paige take a low table near the bar, order glasses of port. The Amazon is a glamazon, Tira says.

I lacked that hard confidence, Paige laughs. She looks into Tira's eyes. But you—you were always a fireball.

At Brown, Tira's first boyfriend was Russell, a management major who bartended on weekends. Tira declined his invitation to a party one night, said she needed to stay in and finish a paper. The paper took less time than anticipated, so she went to his room, slid into his bed, waited to surprise him, and fell asleep.

He didn't see her at first when he came in, nor did the girl with him. They heard Tira's scream. The girl buttoned her shirt as she darted for the door. Tira kept screaming. She threw lamps and books and beer mugs. Russell screamed back, told her she was insane, he hadn't done anything wrong, pointed out that he and Tira weren't even sleeping together yet.

The *yet* really got to her. She screamed because she'd thrown everything in the room she could lift. Their yelling woke half the block. The next morning, everyone on campus had heard the story. Russell became a legend, *the slutty bartender*, a title he managed well.

What makes the story more memorable is the way they

ran into each other in San Francisco more than a decade later. Russell, now a bartender/nightclub investor, invited Tira to a baseball game. She accepted and met Sam.

Their port arrives and Tira does not toast to love or friendship or success. To the squatters, she says, for being in the right place at the right time.

The port tastes bold—sweet and spicy at once.

Paige, not usually the romantic one, thinks how Brian is her right place and time. She recalls the morning she woke to the smell of breakfast, the sounds of Brian's footsteps in the kitchen. A note sat on the bedside table, propped between the lamp and alarm clock. *Feel like getting married?* As she reached for it she saw the diamond ring Brian had slipped on her finger while she slept.

The air outside the restaurant smells of cologne and grilled meat. Tira turns her mobile on, watches the voicemail indicator blink.

If pressed, Paige would admit that her lover's dorky smile endears her, like all of his details. If only he were an image, like a heartthrob in a teen magazine, and not so undeniably real. Brian, in the beginning, had seemed super-human, almost too much for her, a wondrous compilation of muscle, desire, and verve. Her lover seems less distinct. Every time she wants to define him, his description unfurls.

Paige waits in the Gulfstream courtyard while Tira argues with Sam on her mobile. Sam went temperamental on his coach again, told him to fuck off, nearly got kicked off the team. Keep your shit together, Tira warns him, do not mess this up.

Paige sighs. It was supposed to happen only once.

She said yes that first time in Arizona thinking it better to get this attraction out of the way, fearing it would haunt her otherwise. Just once, she told him.

Brian would have laughed at her, would have recalled

the times in restaurants she ordered molten chocolate cake, promising to take only one bite. She would take a measured, careful bite, hesitate, then give in. Just one more time, she would say, and take one last bite again and again until she stared into the center of a white plate.

The very worst part, Paige thinks, was the inability to share the wonder of one with the other. The way she could not say to Brian, the first time, You will never believe what happened to me in Arizona. The way she could not sit down with her lover, the last time, to show photos of her wedding day. A crazy thought, she knows, yet in this moment, she feels completely sane.

Tira tells Sam she loves him and they should talk before he goes to practice in the morning. She says something about attitude, his hot head, tells him that he needs to give her a wake-up call.

They stroll around the plaza outside Gulfstream, decide window-shopping seems safest at midnight when the boutiques are closed. The Doggy Bakery displays a snack-filled basket made of Milkbones. Zany Brainy has red and yellow kites, beach toys, something resembling Erector sets. Subtle Tones shows yellow chenille blankets in the window, matching robes and eye masks. The air feels heavy and moist around them. Paige thinks of the Cove's cottages, how on a night like this, there would have been a bonfire, a guitar, songs.

They're having a girl, Paige says.

Tira stops. How do you know?

My assistant called his assistant regarding a referral, heard all about a pink layette the women in his office were creating for the baby shower.

Wow, Tira says. You're sure your assistant has no idea about him?

Positive, Paige says. You're the only one who knows.

Paige feels lightness in her head, the wine creating a soft hum between her ears.

Tira sighs. Mine is having a girl too.

How do you know?

Ammnio, Tira says. He told me over coffee last week.

Is everything okay? Paige asks.

Yes, but they were at a stage where they were nervous about everything.

The hum in Paige's head becomes a soft drumbeat, then the slow pounding of a hammer. She hears the swish of traffic from MacArthur Boulevard. Somewhere beyond this place they stand, a battle is waged, other women kiss men they shouldn't for the very first time. A deck is being added, a porch enclosed. Paige reaches for Tira's hand.

She looks around the plaza, listens to the pounding of a truck in the distance, wonders how their paths led to this exact moment in their lives.

So two girls, Tira says. Her face softens. The sparkles have left her cheeks.

Two girls, Paige says. She tightens her grip on Tira's hand. They move closer to the boutique window, try to look deeper inside. Tira sees the blood first.

To the left of the window display, a trail of blood moves across the sidewalk toward them. Tira rushes to it, screams to Paige to call 911. Amazon Girl is slumped against the shop door, eyes closed and unconscious, clothing soaked as purple-red blood rushes from gapes in her neck and stomach.

Tira kneels next to her, knees now in a puddle of blood the size of a pillow. Paige says, Be careful, but Tira doesn't hear, yells for Amazon Girl to speak, to say something, *anything, please.* Tira lowers Amazon Girl's shoulders, lays her head quickly and gently on the ground. Tira pulls her own jacket off, tears the sleeves from it. She holds the sleeves at the site of the wound at her neck, but its little help, the blood flow relentless. She presses the rest of her jacket against the stomach wound but the blood seems to devour it. Tira cannot keep back the sobs now as she holds her makeshift bandages, looking for something, anything more she might do.

She has been stabbed, Paige tells the operator quickly, although stabbed seems to be understating it. Paige goes over it a second time for a second operator, but hears already the sirens speeding up PCH. There is just too much blood, Paige cries into the phone. I think so, Paige whispers. She's more certain than that but cannot bear to say so. Her clothing is fastened and one of her shoes is missing, Paige answers. No, I don't see it, she says.

There is no stabbing object in sight. Just blood and more blood.

Tira won't have it, keeps screaming, sobbing, no, *no!* Paige hears people in the distance, people leaving the restaurant, some running toward them. Paige throws the phone down on the sidewalk and moves in closer, kneels next to Tira. She puts her own jacket over Tira's on the stomach wound. Tira continues to apply pressure hoping to stop the blood even though it's too late. Paige hears a man's voice yelling, Don't touch her, stop, back up, crime scene.

Tira removes her hands from Amazon Girl's stomach and feels down her arm to hold her hand. Paige puts her arm around Tira and thinks she is thankful that Amazon Girl's eyes are closed. She notices that her eye shadow glimmers in spite of the world around it. Tira trembles and Paige takes deep breaths to keep from crying harder. The sirens go on. There is a chopper above, the glare of vehicle lights on the store window, more yelling.

It feels like an hour, yet it is only a moment that they sit together this way, their knees firmly planted in this growing pool of blood. They do not leave until police officers pull them away; until the chaos around them blurs.

In the Protection of
Levees

When I arrive in New Orleans, my best friend Sarah is waiting at the airport with fresh beignets. She waves, yells to me in the Big Easy accent that started falling into her voice after four years here. Julianna, she says, welcome. We walk arm and arm through the airport, eat beignets as we wait for my bag to appear on the carousel. Our saying about beignets: they exist simply to get powdered sugar on your face.

The last time I saw Leo we were here, in New Orleans. I met Vance, my fiancé, three months later. Leo was already with the woman who would become his wife, but, conveniently, had yet to tell me. What he told me was that his father was leaving his mother. After thirty-five years, he said, the guy just decides he doesn't want to be married anymore.

We walked down Canal Street, trying to ignore the beginning of rain.

There isn't someone else, he said. My father promised it's not that.

I didn't assume that it was, I said. How is your mom holding up?

His face was as gray as the sky right then. She's not, he said.

I wouldn't be either, I said.

A half hour later we were having sex in the bathroom at Arnaud's, and he said, I think you might. I think you're the one person who might hold up.

The best story assigned in my Senior lit course had this line: *Once he looked at me and I knew he wanted me and I wasn't scared he would stop.* And the first time I read it, I knew I felt the same way about Leo, that this mutual intensity was the thing that made my stomach knot and churn. And I decided in that frilly bathroom at Arnaud's, that whatever that feeling had been, it eluded us now. I knew the way he looked into my eyes, trance-like, that this was goodbye.

I hated him then. I hated that he wasn't saying it in words, that we were standing up, clothes pushed away, not taken off; that I was the one he'd confide in about his family, not the one who'd become part of it. I hated that he saw some strength in me I never saw in myself. I hated in advance the way I would miss him, the way I would dream of him and wake with a start. By the time we came, at the moment my hands were in his hair and his forehead was perspiring onto mine, hate became something else, something stronger, softer, and urgent.

I love you, he said. He tried to catch his breath.

I know, I said.

Sarah and I go to dinner at the New York Club, a gold room full of gray-haired businessmen. We are the youngest people in the room by decades, the only people not talking in estimates, quotes, and options. We arrive early for our reservation because the crab puffs they serve at the bar are irresistible.

It would seem odd to our peers that Sarah and I feel so at home here, in this establishment they would not frequent in a million years. When Sarah and I met, we understood each other's childhoods immediately. We were raised in family businesses. The men we called uncles were not our father's brothers, but their attorneys and accountants. We knew the date of the first day of school, and the end of the fiscal year. Our closets held more dinner clothes than play clothes, and we ate countless meals in places just like this.

My mother's favorite story from my childhood describes the first time she asked me to set the dining room table for Thanksgiving. I put the tablecloth down, then went into the study and grabbed my dad's blueprints. I put them over the table like runners. I was used to eating with them, so I wanted them there.

Sarah and I pop crab puffs into our mouths, drink Bellinis. Men smile and nod at us. Not in a suggestive way—they understand we are not here to cruise way-older men. We seem familiar to them, look vaguely like their own granddaughters, daughters, nieces, or those of their friends.

As we take our seats, the maitre'd, having heard of Sarah's engagement, sends a bottle of champagne to our table. We're both engaged, Sarah says to the wine steward, and he stares for a moment, trying to figure out if we mean to each other. Neither of us wears an engagement ring in the traditional way. My ring is a black diamond solitaire, but the band is too big, so it's on my middle finger for now. Andrew gave Sarah a navel ring with a ruby.

Our friends Natalie and Jenn arrive tomorrow. No bride-y tricks, Sarah promises, no bachelorette party stuff. Just four chickas toasting life partnership, talking, getting our minds away from our jobs to enjoy French food and Spring in New Orleans. No hurricane drinking contests, she says, no penis shaped straws. But I've arrived early because—this is the sort of thing we never thought we'd say—Sarah wants me to help her decide on a china pattern.

The four of us—Sarah, Natalie, Jenn and I—met at Tulane. Sarah stayed in New Orleans after graduation. I went to Los Angeles, Natalie to Seattle, Jenn to Chicago.

After we've taken our first sips of champagne, Sarah says it: Being here all weekend is going to remind you of Leo, isn't it?

There are black and white drawings of New Orleans and New York scenes in gold frames above our table and all over the room. The histories of these great cities are more tied than people think. New Orleans' setting, on a curve of the Mississippi River, defies logic. Sarah holds her champagne glass near her chest, looks down at the bubbles.

Maybe, but this weekend is about you, I say, about friendship, future.

She raises her right eyebrow at me. She knows how we over-analyze relationships, even when they're in the past. Sarah has made her home here in New Orleans. She understands how haunting this place can be.

Really, I'm fine, I say. And I think I mean it.

The thing about New Orleans is this: It depends on the protection of levees. It amazes us to feel anything but vulnerability here.

Sarah and I take off for Macy's in the morning. In the car, she says she cannot decide between Royal Doulton's Broadway, Haviland's Gotham, or something-or-other Paladium. Andrew doesn't care what color china they eat from for the rest of their lives, and she never though she would either, but somehow she does.

They've got me, she says, the whole capitalist wedding regime. *I swear, they use the grooms' whack mothers as henchwomen, get them to throw around those wedding books and magazines. So to be a good sport, you give in and read one, and it's like a drug. It's like you've swallowed the entire apothecary chest. Your head spins, and you want to register for demitasse cups, but you can't decide if you really need eight or twelve, and you sacrifice an entire work day fretting about it. Suddenly you want bows around chairs at your reception, and you want little silk bags around disposable cameras, and you want a guest book with lace trim for everyone to sign. And then you say, What the hell am I doing here? I wanted to do important things with my life. I wanted to help starving children. Then you feel this guilt about having a life that condones fretting about demitasse cups, bows, bags, and lace, when children all over the world are without drinking water, global warming is ruining the Arctic, the Dalai Lama is still in exile—you get my point. Please tell me you know what I'm talking about. I think it's like your attacks of the soul in school.*

I nod. Yes, it is exactly like that, I tell her.

Sarah's car smells like coffee beans.

At Tulane, there were nights when I couldn't go out. I'd think, here we go, drinking slushy drinks, wearing beads and dancing as if all the world's a party, when the world is completely corrupt and fucked up. I'd decide to stay home in bed to worry about Earth.

Natalie would come by my room to say, There's nothing we can do about all of that tonight, sweetie, so we might as well have a drink. Jenn would say, you know, I've been thinking how sociology probably *is* the major for you. When I switched to journalism, Jenn said, Another heartbreaker—this isn't going to be any better.

Don't worry, I tell Sarah. And I confess: I bought a copy of *Modern Bride* and read it in traffic so that I could pitch it in a recycling bin in the alley before I went home. I didn't want Vance to think I'd gone Barbie on him.

Did it make you want bows? Sarah said.

My answer disappoints her. It made me decide to elope, I say.

Sarah holds up her index finger to interrupt me, to answer her cell phone. It strikes me as odd now that one of the first things a bride does is select china. Something so fragile and fleeting. Bone china in a city of bone yards.

How about pewter instead, I say, when Sarah finishes her call. She shakes her head. China, she says, smiles, and looks around for a parking space. It has to be fine china.

At the entrance to Macy's there are miniature silver picture frames full of gold and white beads wrapped in tiny see-through boxes.

Wow, Sarah says. This is what you need to do with your Leo memories.

She picks up a box and waves it around for affect.

This is exactly it. You need to wrap them in a tiny little box and put them away with the stuff you're not sure why you had in the first place.

Maybe I already did that, I want to say. But Sarah's right. Leo is still with me, because as I laugh, I think about the way he would have rolled his eyes at Sarah's little show.

One afternoon last fall, Vance and I were poking around Century City Mall looking for an anniversary gift for his parents. Bloomingdale's had this gorgeous display of dinnerware. Green mugs surrounded stacks of huge purple plates, towers of gold and burgundy bowls. On top of one of the plates sat a bronze creamer, triangular, and the way the light hit made it sparkle. A large, bald man who'd also been browsing around the department—he and Vance had exchanged confused glances in front of a display of soup tureens—reached up to touch the creamer. As his finger touched the handle, ever so slightly, the entire display came crashing down. Broken pieces flew around us like sparks.

The crash, it's echo, the children from the nearby toy department screaming in response, the colorful shards flying everywhere—for that moment I was a little girl watching the most brilliant fireworks display. It seemed amazing, a pottery storm in vivid color. Then I noticed the look on the man's face, startled, defeated.

A saleswoman came running toward us saying, God damned it, I told them a flimsy little table would never hold a display like that. Thank God no one is hurt.

But the man didn't hear her. He was muttering, and we couldn't make out what he was saying, until he said, I'm so sorry, I have no idea why I touched. It was such a mistake.

It's not your fault, I told him. It came down like a Jenga game, Vance said.

It's okay, sir, really, the salesperson said. Pieces of mugs crunched under her feet as she moved toward him. And he stood there for the longest time, staring at the debris.

When Jenn and Natalie arrive at Sarah's house, they have a card for Andrew that says, *In sickness and in health and in spite of all the weird friends that come with the deal.*

He's going to love this, Sarah says.

Natalie has cut her hair. It's my British neo-punk phase, she jokes. Natalie has no idea how gorgeous she is, detests the freckles that only make her beauty more intense.

Jenn—who has been anti-cosmetic the entire time we've known her—appears to be wearing mascara. We have to get to the bottom of that, Natalie teases.

Hey, Jenn says, it's just gunk on a wand.

Jenn is the quiet one, the cynical and wise one. Natalie says she is like a French voter—not so easily swayed. The four of us have become a sort of family. Since we've left home, our actual families have broken, become distracted. The stories of our families are long ones, but what we've discovered is this: The tale of one broken family, at its core, is not so different from that of the next.

Sarah points to her navel and the sparkling ruby that adorns it. No way, Natalie says. It's so you, Jenn says. In our neo-family, when one of us has news the other three fly into town. It's an unspoken arrangement, the way we live together even when apart. When Jenn got a huge and unexpected promotion, we raced to Chicago with concert plans and shopping guides. At this moment in our lives, the blessing is that our friendships defy geography.

Cheaptickets.com loves us, Natalie joked. Natalie dated a guy at Amazon.com, met lots of big dot-comers, knew all the cool sites. When I'd recommend a book, she'd buy it for all of us with her boyfriend's discount. Eventually their relationship tanked. We flew to Seattle with cookies and sleeping bags and all the slumber party ingredients.

We're way cooler than Amazon Guy, we told her, and you've still got us. She pointed out the window to the place on her street where his motorcycle left tread marks.

When Vance and I got engaged three months ago, Jenn, Natalie, and Sarah fluttered into Los Angeles. They'd made spa appointments in celebration. Yay, Sarah yelled when she saw me at the airport. She ran off the Jetway smiling so hard her cheeks might have burst.

Jenn and Natalie couldn't hide their surprise, their relief. Vance is exactly right for you, they said. And thank God, they said. They had predicted that somehow, even though it seemed so twisted, or wrong, I'd end up with Leo.

At Tulane, Jenn was the one with vision, the one we trusted to keep us sane. Leo is a jerk, she said the day she met him. You don't see it, but he is. I hate the way he seems so disinterested in everything, she said. What she was really saying was, she hated that he would become disinterested in me.

Leo and I would attend parties together, but we'd talk to friends and classmates on the opposite sides of rooms all evening and I'd end up convinced that another woman had fascinated him, that he'd forgotten I was there.

Then he'd grab me in a hallway or kitchen and he'd put his breath to my ear, his hands at my hips, and tell me I'd been driving him crazy, that he hadn't been concentrating in any of his conversations. My aura had distracted—once he said *dismantled*—him.

Later, when we were alone, he'd know specific gestures I had made, the way I had laughed with someone, or tiled my head. It felt spooky. But it also felt magnetic and sexy. Perhaps we could have only happened here, in this city of contradictions, a place that based its compass on the bend in a river.

I told Natalie then how my favorite short story reminded me of Leo. I did not specify that it was because the story's narrator says, *The only way I can get over him is if I die. I don't die.*

Freshman year, Jenn arrived at our Tulane dormitory wearing a vintage dress, Birkenstocks, her hair frizzed out, no makeup. Our resident advisor took one look at her and said, New Orleans is a tough place for a feminist. Without missing a beat Jenn said, then I'll be a tough feminist for New Orleans.

We loved her from that day forward. Sarah thinks we are the perfect family because there are four of us. If there were two, we would compete. With three, someone would always feel left out, and with five or more, it would be far too difficult to keep track of each other. Four, she insists, is the ideal number.

That first year at Tulane, our resident advisor was a teaching assistant at Newcomb College Center for Research on Women. She knew great stories about old New Orleans. She took us to the balcony of the Bourbon Orleans Hotel. In the early 1800s the balcony, covered, had been the Quadroon Ballroom.

Quadroon was the name given to people whose racial makeup was one quarter African, and young quadroon women were said to possess legendary beauty. A French man would come to the ballroom, select his favorite woman, and with her mother's approval, buy her a lavish house and support her as his mistress. The arrangement included guarantees that children of these unions would be sent to France to be educated.

Natalie felt fascinated by the Quadroon Balls and read everything about them she could find. Do you remember? I ask.

We're sitting on loungers outside Café Brazil drinking lemonade with vodka. It's freakishly warm for a spring afternoon.

Barely, Natalie says. I probably stopped reading those things to hang out with Badass Number One.

Amazon Guy has been crowned Badass Number Two. Natalie reunited with him for a while, but hasn't seen him since the last break. When she called to tell me they'd ended it again, she said, You know, that entire time we could have been supporting independent booksellers.

What are we reading next? Jenn wants to know.

Yeah, Sarah says, and we laugh. Always Sarah reads the first chapter, the last, then guesses the middle. Sometimes her middle is more dramatic than the real one.

New Orleans sits like a saucer, more than six feet below sea level. The Mississippi River serves as a southern boundary, until it dips and cuts into the city near the French Quarter. As students, sometimes we'd walk near the river on Saturday afternoons. When the water was high, we looked out to passing ships and noticed them traveling above our heads. When the water was low, we tried to make out the levees themselves, the huge bricks of black earth that formed the city's fortress.

When I was fourteen years old, my closest friend died. She'd been home from school five days with flu-like symptoms. Everyone thought she'd be fine. She and I talked on the phone every day after General Hospital and homework. The very last time I spoke to her, there was a special about Third Eye Blind on MTV. We watched it on the phone together. That night, sitting at her family's dinner table in her nightgown, she suffered heart failure.

Like the kids around me, I had no idea how to process that, so for some time we resembled zombies. Eventually life crept back into our faces, and every boy I liked during the next two years told me how he'd wanted to ask my friend out, how he thinks he was in love with her when she died.

We all loved her, I would say.

Other girls got the same stories from their boys. So it amazes me now, in those years of grief, eating and sleeping disorders, and sexual cravings, that none of us offed ourselves. That year my town had the highest number of rainy days on record. The weeks grew longer and darker and the message we kept getting again and again was everyone loves a dead girl.

There were moments after she died when I thought, how is it possible to miss someone this much? I'd have an urge to run until I couldn't anymore, to pound my feet into the ground and sprint until I fell from exhaustion. At first I felt alone, even though I wasn't exactly. With my peers, I grew up in the presence of this strange absence.

Before I met Vance, I kept thinking Leo was the life I was supposed to have, the route I was meant to go. Maybe, as people all over the world were dying, I kept crying and making wrong turns. One time I asked Vance if I lean on him too much. That's ridiculous, he said. You don't lean on me enough. You keep too much inside.

The night before my friend died she told me a secret. She was planning to break up with her boyfriend. He had gone to boarding school while she had stayed home. She worried they would miss too much if they couldn't date other people. We were fourteen years old, so this kind of talk was new and huge.

I'd promised not to say a word, that it was our secret. I never told anyone, ever. Not even the girl who made out with my friend's boyfriend the weekend after, when he had traveled home for the funeral. She felt awful about it, begged me to say something, anything, to make her feel better. All I could do was shrug my shoulders, explain that really, there was nothing to say.

Tourists seem endlessly fascinated by New Orleans cemeteries. The first French settlers held traditional burials for their loved ones, until flood waters brought the coffins up, allowed coffins to glide around like boats. So they developed elaborate aboveground tombs, homes to keep their bones at rest. It is the first thing I loved about New Orleans—the way the dead are not held in the earth; they continue share its surface with the living.

The four of us stroll the French Quarter drinking café au lait from paper cups with cardboard sleeves. You'd think we'd tire of these streets, Jenn says. But we never do.

There really is a streetcar named Desire, but it's retired. Desire Street kept its name for a hundred years, but a bus replaced the streetcar. *A Bus Route Named Desire* never had the same appeal, Jenn liked to say. Tourists keep revealing themselves by calling the cars trolleys.

Watch where you're walking, Sarah says, there's glass on the sidewalk.

Before Andrew, Sarah wanted to date all kinds of men, called herself the Sampler. Because of Vance's work on a documentary about the house music, I keep thinking of the music term sampling—when a performer takes part of another artist's song and makes it part of his own.

Perhaps I had taken Leo in those last trips to New Orleans. He hadn't said it, but I knew he had a woman in Washington. It was the sort of deep-soul knowing that skips right over suspicion. There is no process to it. You don't know, and suddenly you do. So in those final moments, maybe I had taken another woman's man, and for the course of a song, made him my own.

Julianna, Sarah says. I snap back to attention as I'm about to walk straight into a parking meter. Jenn and Natalie are on their cell phones, talking to their offices.

Sarah tries not to laugh. Lost in thoughts, she says. Maybe it's time for a boozy drink.

Jenn and Natalie keep talking into their phones.

Come on girls, Sarah screams, it's Saturday.

Jenn works for Planned Parenthood, and the rest of us work in systems. Natalie is a systems consultant; Sarah is a systems coordinator; and I am a systems analyst. We have ever-changing job descriptions which none of us can articulately explain. Reports, goals, strategies. McWorld careers, Jenn says. Just once, we tease, we want Jenn to wear a suit to work.

As we walk, I tell Sarah that we have to make certain promises. We have to promise not to subscribe to *InStyle Weddings*, not to make our friends wear meringue. And in return, they merely have to leave phones and gadgets at home on our wedding days.

Sarah sighs. Here's the thing, she says. I've been to the boutiques. I know I've only been engaged a week, but I just couldn't wait. The very best bridesmaids dresses really are in pink, I swear.

Jenn and Natalie end their calls, turn their attention. Did you hear that? I ask.

Well, I think everyone looks good in pink, Natalie says. Her cheeks have flushed from wind and caffeine.

Watch where you're walking, Sarah says. More glass.

Jenn rolls her eyes, laughs. I knew it, she says. Why do I think you're only moments away from telling us what length to cut our hair; that we must paint our toenails in a color called Ballet Slipper?

Julianna, what about your wedding? Natalie wants to know.

I'm eloping, or we're all wearing black, I tell them. We can't decide.

Natalie got kicked out of Tulane during our junior year. Sarah, Jenn, and I had gone on Spring Break in the Bahamas. Natalie stayed in New Orleans to be near the badass guy she'd been hot on. We came back from the islands, tanned and hung over, to find letters from Natalie, at home in San Francisco, saying she'd spent only one night in jail, so that was lucky, but she'd been expelled from the university indefinitely.

He said he loved me, she explained, so I stole car parts.

We understood completely.

Natalie's father serves as an honorary consulate to France. Before her expulsion, when Natalie's parents visited her, we would go to The Red Room. Each piece of the original Paris restaurant, which had been tucked inside the Eiffel Tower, was sent to New Orleans by ship and reassembled by Creole artisans.

On the night of her arrest in New Orleans, Natalie's parents were in Paris dining at an event for President Chirac and his family. The police, in their condescending southern way, said, It would be best if we could speak to your parents, young lady.

They're in France, Natalie said, having dinner with the president.

Yeah, yeah, the chief said. And my wife is in England, having tea with the queen. Just get them on the phone, young lady.

So Natalie had no choice but to call her eighty-year-old grandfather, at home in San Francisco, asleep in his Pacific Heights co-op. When the police finished with him and handed the phone to Natalie he said, Jesus, honey, car parts? If you had asked really nicely I'm sure your dad would have helped you buy an entire car.

As we wander the French Quarter, Natalie stops into various shops to buy *gris-gris* for friends back in Seattle. Jenn announces she has a new cat. Another goddess name? Sarah asks. Jenn's current cats are Aphrodite and Athena.

This time I went with a God, Jenn says.

Sarah and I look at her, impressed.

The cat's name is Michael Vartan, Jenn tells us.

Who is that? Sarah says, just as I'm about to ask the same.

He's the actor who plays the hot CIA handler on the hit show *Alias*. She says *the hit show Alais* like a television announcer.

Since when do you watch television? Sarah wants to know.

Since I moved to a city capable of a twenty-below-zero wind chill factor in the spring, Jenn says.

Natalie comes out of Voodoo Lounge with a shopping bag.

I just told them about Michael Vartan, Jenn says.

Natalie laughs. I think the world must really be coming to an end, she says. You two are getting married, Jenn named a cat for a man...

And took up mascara, I say. Jenn swats me.

And I'm sleeping with a guy who is not a badass, Natalie announces.

Oh my God, Sarah screams, you've been holding out on us. Tell us right now.

It's the phone guy, Natalie says. We stop walking, stand together at the corner of Chartres and Barracks.

As in your phone repairman? I ask.

No, as in the guy who designs cell phones for Eriksson.

Holy shit, Sarah says.

As in that guy from Denmark, I say, the one in all the tech magazines?

That's him, Natalie sings.

Oh my God, Sarah says, holy shit. She shakes her head, stunned.

Natalie laughs. Her cheeks go from pink to red. That's the one, she says.

His designs really are revolutionary, Jenn says, more than a little in awe.

Believe me, Natalie says, giggling like a schoolgirl, he is extremely talented.

They say New Orleans is home of the quintessential love affair. The day I arrived at my Tulane dorm, I saw a man at the entrance dressed as Cupid, standing on a red box, shooting arrows toward men on the Quad.

Look, Natalie said, climbing the steps with a giant suitcase. We had yet to meet but we'd arrived at the same time. He's going to shoot all of the good ones for himself.

The first two years we met random eager boys and their sloppy kisses at Carnival. We went on coffee dates that led nowhere with more serious types. And once in a while there would be dorm sex with a good one.

By junior year, Natalie had the badass, and Jenn fell in love with a drummer who tested her limits by becoming a stockbroker. In our final year, Sarah decided she'd date artistically. That's when the Sampler thing started. It means she dates in turbo, Jenn liked to say.

For me there was Leo, a grad student, and not so much a relationship as an ill-timed affair, a thing that started as we were about to leave for our next cities.

Leo and I thought only for a moment about staying in New Orleans, convinced ourselves it could work from wherever we were. Lots of people have long distance things, I said. We made promises that we wouldn't dwindle to occasional weekend sex fests, wouldn't let it fizzle to something insignificant. So we would search for bargain fares on Expedia to visit one another, or try to coordinate a rendezvous with our business travel.

We were together in Washington, Los Angeles, Houston, and New Orleans, and New Orleans three times more. In Washington he said, We're going to have to really try. In Los Angeles he said, It's hard, but we have to keep trying. In Houston, we said nothing, ate nothing. We couldn't keep our hands off each other long enough to create a conversation or take in a meal. In New Orleans he said, I'm not sure I'm ever going to be able to get you out of my system. And then I couldn't deny it: the thing he had been trying at was an ending, not a beginning.

The first friend I made in Los Angeles was Cody, a program line-ups director at Paragon Entertainment. Cody was between boyfriends and had yet to come out at work. When a Paragon Executive invited the entire staff to a holiday party at his home in Pacific Palisades, Cody needed a safety date.

It's not that I'm avoiding the coming out thing, Cody said. I just don't want to go to the trouble for some guy I met in a bar and dragged to a holiday party. When I agreed to go, Cody said, I'd wear the lavender dress if I were you. And a wrap. And what are you thinking of doing with your hair?

I wore it up. When we arrived at the host's home—a three story Mediterranean in a gated community—men in suits kept kissing my cheeks, saying, You must be the one who makes those irresistible little muffins Cody keeps bringing to the office.

Yes, Cody kept saying, nudging me to go along, this is my Julianna.

Remind me to kill you later, Mr. Martha Stewart, I whispered to him.

That's when we noticed Vance. He was the safety date of a woman named Barb who hadn't come out either. He had brown eyes, and the slightest bit of curl in his dark hair. He had a square jaw, and when he smiled a dimple appeared in his right cheek and not his left. That little lack of symmetry made my knees weak.

If he's gay, he's mine, Cody said the moment we saw him. I can't tell—my gaydar must be off tonight. Mine isn't, I said. He's got to be straight. There are two billion butterflies racing around my stomach. Maybe it's the crudités, Cody said. It's not the crudités, I told him.

Cody and I ignored trays of mini quiches, mini crab cakes, and mini stuffed tomatoes and watched him for two hours. We noticed how shy he seemed, which made us feel shy as we tried to concoct a plan to approach him. Then we saw him throw his leather jacket over his arm and move toward the door. No way, I said.

He can't leave, Cody said. Cody's jaw dropped. He looked at me in horror.

Before I realized what he was doing, Cody took the olive from his martini and flung it across the room with perfect aim so that it slapped Vance in the back of the head. Vance turned, grinned in our direction, but continued toward the door.

Damned, Cody said. He grabbed the olive out of my martini sending half of the drink onto my dress. Don't worry, he said, I have a great dry cleaner.

With near-perfect aim, he shot again. This time the olive missed, but swiped past Vance's left temple at lightning speed so he couldn't help but notice.

Vance turned, grinning again. His dimple appeared as he walked toward us.

Hooked him, Cody said, now reel him in, sister.

As we walk the bend on Chartres the serious look creeps onto Sarah's face again. Natalie and Jenn have stopped several feet behind us to read a posted menu outside a new café.

I know something new, Sarah says. She sighs. I just heard this morning. Andrew knows someone who knows Leo. Her voice trails off. The story is, well, his parents are back together, but he's getting a divorce. His wife moved out after the first few months.

Sarah stares, unsure how I'll react. I thought you should know. I'm not exactly numb to the news, or overwhelmed by it. There's a notable lack of wonder. The only thing I feel is sorry. I'm sorry for him, I say. And I mean it. But it doesn't change anything for me.

We walk further. Oh, this city of bone yards, I say to myself.

When Natalie and Jenn catch up to us, they look serious too. Jenn sighs. Everything is going to change, she says. She pulls her hair off her face into a ponytail holder. Natalie nods.

Nothing has to change, Sarah says, and she says the words quickly, to get them out before she realizes they're not true.

A year before my friend died, she and I found the new girl, Rosalinda, crying in the bathroom at school. It's the boys, she said. Rosalinda had come from an all-girls school, wasn't used to boy bullies. She sniffled in all the tears she could manage, said, They saw me eating the green M&Ms.

It was an old joke, one that had been with us since fifth grade. The boys started saying that girls who ate green M&Ms were horny. And we were so scared of words like horny that for years we'd been leaving the green ones at the bottom of the bag. Rosalinda had thrown three green M&Ms into her mouth during study hall, and the harassment began.

One of the boys coughed the word slut into his hands, then the word whore came from three directions, and one bolder, dirtier boy said, I'll do you, baby, and then the football players joined in the commentary.

As I handed Rosalinda a tissue from my bag, my best friend told her to stick with us for the rest of the day, to meet us at the football game that night. We arrived for the game early, sat in the middle stands, and my friend called out to other girls in our class, Hey Becky, sit with us; Rhonda, come here; Melanie, we're saving a seat for you.

When all of the girls were seated together, and the boys were checking us out from their places in the stands, and halftime had come, so the players were looking too, my friend opened her knapsack and pulled out dozens of quart size Ziploc bags filled entirely with green M&Ms.

She passed them out and we all laughed and ate green M&Ms by the fistful. We crunched loudly, as if ravenous, and followed my friend's lead by looking at the boys straight-on, daring them, and watching, for the first time, the fear appear on their faces. It was the smallest of victories, but big enough to keep Rosalinda from more tears; to remind us the value of girls sticking together.

When my train of marriage thoughts takes me to New Orleans, I realize the city's darkness is about more than restlessness. Likely those Southern ghosts simply possess residual energy, awe, or joy. Maybe they don't mean to defy—they just have some extra living to do. The concept of marriage fills me with surprise and wonder, with a loving sense of the dead. I think of my lost friend and devotion so strong that the loss of it impales your heart.

Each time I write the word *married* on my computer, I misspell it. *Marriend*, I write. And I only see it that way for a moment. Microsoft Word fixes the gaff for me with a flash of red. It corrects so quickly that I almost miss the poetry of it; that I have ended this word with end. I say I am getting merry end.

I didn't need to die to get over Leo. I only needed to see, recognize, and remember the things healthier than obsession. With Leo I'd forgotten too much. I kept overflowing.

Vance knew, even before I told him, that I had lost someone. We'd finished a bottle of wine lounging on the sofa at my Los Angeles apartment, and he'd touched my cheek, and I'd smiled and somehow the smile took him by surprise. That's nice, he said. I hope you'll do that more. And I must have stared at him then. He said there was a deep inner sadness in me, and I nodded, and he pulled me into his arms.

The china pattern Sarah picks has four evenly spaced gold diamonds. If you look at the dinner plate from a distance the diamonds seem to be connected by four blue lines. As you move closer, you realized the lines aren't lines at all, but collections of individual blue dots.

When the afternoon winds down we relax at Sarah's house, all four of us lying across her bed, overlapping like fallen dominoes. Andrew is off with friends, presumably to give us what he calls our *girl time*. Natalie lies partly under Sarah. She is loopy, sappy, telling Sarah how much we love her. More than the whitest puffiest cloud in the sky, she says, more than pralines, Creole tomatoes, or warm beignets.

Tell us something about Los Angeles, Sarah says. She lies partly under me. White curtains flutter in the heavy breeze. Her room smells like lavender.

It's bright, I say.

Something about Chicago and Seattle, Sarah says.

It's humid, Jenn says. It's wet, Natalie says.

Now New Orleans, I say.

We should wake early tomorrow, Sarah says. It's most inspiring at 6 a.m.

I feel a chill in my shoulders, a good chill, and for a moment I think my fourteen-year-old friend is with us somehow, watching, approving. I want to say to her that this adulthood thing seems different than we predicted, although I no longer remember our predictions exactly. I want to say that I am glad she is here, no matter what form her presence takes.

Gift boxes sit on top of Sarah's dresser, engagement presents from her co-workers.

Jenn sits up from her place on top, looks over to Natalie.

Tell us something about Jacques Chirac that you've never told us before. Natalie thinks for a moment.

President or not, he is less interesting than the women he loves.

Now Jenn looks at Sarah, at me. Her eyes at this moment are as vivid as the leaves on a rosebush.

Tell us something about Andrew and Vance.

Blink and Release Me

My mother-in-law may be in cardiac arrest, and her daughters blame me. We're all fidgeting in an orange waiting room in a New Jersey hospital. Doctors examine her in a special unit on another floor. You just had to upset her, didn't you? Mary Elizabeth says.

I think we've been here a long time, but I'm not sure. It's Christmas. Mary Elizabeth, the oldest sister, wears her mother's cardigan and scowl. There is no way to say this without sounding like a bitch: Mary Elizabeth, Mary Margaret, and Mary Constance are offensively dull, and not just because they're named after nuns.

Their husbands have fallen asleep. Mine pretends to read the newspaper. They shouldn't have had the hot buttered rum, Mary Constance says. She is the youngest, an especially tragic case. Only the permanent puss on her face, while not as distinct as a scowl, keeps her from fading into walls.

The thing is, my very existence upsets my mother-in-law. I didn't have to say a thing. Earlier today she pulled my thirty-year-old husband onto her lap as she spoke to him. Later she sat on his. And she scooted deep into his lap. I thought, I am the only one in this room who should have any contact with his lap region. Her behavior would make even the most ardent anti-Freudians flinch.

You should have come to New Jersey without me, I told my husband later, in the car to the hospital.

You're reading too much into this, he said

My husband's mother, when she says goodbye to him on the phone, tells him she loves him. She never did that before we were married, he tells me. She never used to say that at all.

The Marys are making deep sighs, little grunts. They're having a bitter moment. Mary means bitter in Hebrew. It figures, Mary Margaret says to my husband, that you'd marry someone so outspoken and lawless. You always have to stir things up.

I laugh. It's more of a cranky laugh than it should be. If Mary Margaret had said that anywhere but the hospital, in any scenario but this, I would have cracked up in her face. My husband is a puppy. A mini-muffin. He couldn't stir if his life depended on it. My cousin, Brooke—now there's someone with some spice. She could show these Marys a thing or two.

I look in my handbag for my bag of carob chips, my present sweet-tooth addiction. Magazines keep calling carob *the ass-flavored chocolate substitute*, but the magazines are wrong—a much more pleasant possibility than liking the taste of ass.

Actually, the first time my husband and I drank together, he had way too much and admitted his ex-girlfriend obsessed on performing analingus. They must have used a dental dam or something; nonetheless his pet name for her was Butt-Licker-Lana and she liked the name too. My mother-in-law would have a heart attack if she knew.

Oh wait. She is having a heart attack. Or maybe not. When we were alone the car, my husband said, Don't worry, it's just indigestion or stress. You know how she is.

What he means is, you can't be that uptight your whole life

without something bursting at some point. But he would never say it like that. He throws his newspaper aside. A headline about killer bees glares up at us. He is devoted to his mother in spite of that fact that she is a total bitch to me.

Well, I never, my mother-in-law said earlier, in her gray plaid living room. The timed lights of the Christmas tree clicked on. She moved her hands into angry, shaking fists. I had asked her to remove herself from my husband's lap.

This is my home, she said. You simply cannot speak to me in that tone.

The creepy, talking, rotating Santa on top of the tree turned to me and said *Ho* just once because it was broken.

I am your husband's mother, she said, as if I could have forgotten.

I folded my arms, stared. I wasn't apologizing or backing down.

You heard me, I told her. And if she had continued with her *Well, I never*s instead of grabbing her chest, I would have spelled it out for her: *I don't care who you are. You are too close to my husband's dick.*

My father would find my mother-in-law unbearable. My father is in jail. Having dinner at Sarabeth's Kitchen the night before his sentence began, I told him there would be lots of girls where he was going, and he should give them fatherly advice.

Actually, the girls' jails are next door, my father said.

He has a good chin, a strong one.

On the last night of my father's freedom, he said he didn't want to see me at the jail on the first visiting day. He'd rather receive a postcard. Go on to Madrid, he insisted, get out of New York and fall in love.

We had been saving up. Madrid was his birthplace, and he regretted that he'd never taken me there. He wanted me to see for myself how it had grown in uneven and unplanned leaps.

You don't gawk at Madrid, he said. You live it.

I'd been in Madrid only three hours when I met my lover. Restless, I walked the city, and near the Vista Alegra metro, I noticed three Brits arguing. One had *entradas* to enter the bullfight, another was eager to go, and my lover refused. He compared the bullfight to the slaughterhouse, went on and on about ethics. I must have lingered too long as I passed them.

He turned to me, stopped his friend mid-sentence, said perhaps their eavesdropper had an opinion: Was the bullfight an art form or cruel spectacle?

Why can't it be both things? I asked them.

His friends rushed toward the arena while he and I walked toward a café, ordered espresso. I hadn't slept on the plane. In fact, I'd hardly slept in weeks. We talked in the dark café for hours, my words coming slower in spite of the caffeine. In those first moments of getting to know him, I must have been trying so hard to keep my own eyes open that I failed to notice the intensity of his. When he finally took my hand, I rubbed my palm into his and thought, I want to shrink down to miniature size and fall asleep inside this hand.

I excused myself, said I must get to bed immediately.

How long will you stay in Madrid? he wanted to know.

Until I run out of energy or money, I said, whichever comes first.

He told me later that he'd loved that answer.

My lover had this way of looking. It was like his eyes wouldn't let me go even if the rest of him did. He would look into my eyes, and say he couldn't believe how much I blinked. He rarely blinked, and it was freakish. Blinking keeps your eyes clean, I'd tell him. Eyelids are like windshield wipers, I'd remind him.

I think it's more honest, he said, to just look through the *schmutz*.

You remind me of someone, I told him, but I didn't say it was my father.

My husband's father had his heart attack just before we married. He came out of surgery at the hospital next to this one, and the doctor said his chances had gone from twenty percent to zero. I started sobbing. I couldn't help myself—I just lost it, right there in front of everyone.

The Marys looked at me in horror. Can you get her to calm down? one of them asked my husband, a look of utter confusion across her face.

She barely knew him, another said.

But he was a father, I said.

Is she always so emotional? my mother-in-law wanted to know. My husband didn't respond. Emotional people make this sort of thing so hard, she said.

My husband said nothing, but I thought of my lover then, how he wouldn't have blinked.

I'm not supposed to be thinking of myself right now, in the orange buzz of this waiting room on Christmas, but it occurs to me that I need a two-month Buddhist retreat to recover from two days with them. I take a deep breath, look at my husband.

She'll be okay, he whispers.

I keep looking. The waiting room chairs get brighter and brighter. I'd put my sunglasses on if I had them, even though it would make me look like a total quack. Her father is in jail you know, one of the Marys' husbands would whisper to another.

Butt-Licker-Lana was two years before Madrid and they thought she was awful too. I sit and think about Lana. What did she look like? What is she doing now? What would happen if she burst through the waiting room door this very moment?

Until I run out of energy or money, I said in Spain, whichever comes first. My husband hated that answer. My lover and I met my husband at the front desk of my inn, complaining about his room. When we shook hands, he smiled at me and a charge ran thought my body, took me by surprise. This is really fucked up, I thought. I'm in the middle of Madrid with a British lover, somehow attracted to a persnickety New Yorker. My lover noticed my flushed face and looked amused.

Actually, I'm from New Jersey, my husband explained.

You're going to make a very big mistake here, my lover whispered in my ear.

For the next few weeks I was attracted to one, but more comfortable with the other. I no longer know which thing I felt for which man at which time. Morning, nights, dancers, and partners all blend together in Madrid. Moments become more important than distinctions.

I wasn't ready to leave the vibrant red haze of it all, the stuff that inspires flamenco. But my husband wanted to go home, asked me to go with him. He missed his work, his American coffee and TV shows. He loved New York and was not sure why his friends were always telling him to take a break. At first I thought I would stay behind, but when I tried to imagine waking up thousands of air miles away from him, I got sick, started dry heaving. My husband sat against the bathroom wall, held my hair. That settles it, he said.

The carob I brought from the city becomes the only food in my mother-in-law's house that I can stomach. Maybe it's all the pig, I think. My mother-in-law and the Marys and their husbands eat an insane amount of bacon. My mother-in-law saw my carob bag, rolled her eyes, and commented to her daughters that after twenty-five, one is supposed to give up snacking.

On the plane from Madrid to New York, my husband and I made promises. As we settled into a little Chelsea studio, he said he couldn't wait to introduce me to his mother. She chose the New Jersey restaurant where we'd meet. It's a nice place, she told me on the phone, so remind him to wear a jacket.

He wore a black jacket, and I wore a little black dress with low heels. We were ridiculously overdressed. The restaurant was a dive owned by a former baseball announcer, filled with fans in torn jeans with Mets and Giants shirts. It did have cloth napkins, but they were pulled through holes in the middle of mangy old baseballs. I thought I was going to die when she insisted we say grace right there in the restaurant, right in the middle of the sports fans. Out-of-place dark clothing and mumbling to Jesus— we look like a cult, I thought to myself.

I drank too much water and kept leaving to go to the bathroom. Every time I returned to the table, they stopped talking abruptly. His father was there too, but he didn't say a word, didn't make a sound, gesture, or facial expression. He seemed to go into some sort of trance. When we got back to our new apartment, I was about to say, God, that was awful. But my husband hugged me, said, Hey, that went so well.

I threw my purse down and collapsed into our new sofa.

Your mother never cracked a smile.

My husband shook his head, looked confused.

And you talked about me every time I went to the bathroom, I continued. She wanted to know what you were doing with a woman whose father is in prison, right?

No, he said, plopping to the sofa, putting his arm around me. No, no, no. She liked you. She was fine about your father. She remembered him from the news, said she understands he's only in one of those country club prisons. She said her third cousin, a tax evader, went to a place just like it. She thinks it was an important time for him.

My husband said he didn't even have to get into it, to explain anything.

She called my father's prison a country club? I pulled away. They don't exactly have golf, tennis, or shuffleboard, I said. It occurred to me that actually the might have shuffleboard, but I wasn't about to correct myself.

She had only one complaint, my husband went on. He lowered his head. The new sofa smelled like pine. He was nervous at that moment and blinking a lot.

Oh God, I said. It's religion, isn't it?

Well probably that too, but mainly the piercings, he said, smirking.

That's ridiculous, I told him. I'm wearing a dress. There is absolutely no way she saw my navel rings.

Earrings, he said.

Excuse me.

She thinks gypsy pierce their ears.

He laughed, but this wasn't a joke.

She doesn't really understand why you would call your lineage into question with those earrings, you know, those gypsy things. He laughed and went on, something about her praying for me, but I didn't hear the rest. He'd gotten ahead.

Wait, I said. I'm wearing the most fucking conservative earrings I own—they don't even dangle. Jackie O. wore earrings, I said. Fucking everyone wears earrings.

I was shouting. I should have probably been an ounce or two amused, but I was angry, and there was more to it than jewelry. My anger felt too complex to get a grip on. I took a deep breath, tried to center. None of the Marys have pierced ears? I wanted to know.

He gave me his look, hated when I grouped his sisters together like that. My sisters are individuals, he told me once.

But after I met them I realized he'd been trying to convince himself as well as me.

Actually, no, he said. His face hardened. Really honey, this is good, he said, even better than I expected.

Of course there were other things. They filtered down through the Marys. I had the wrong age, attitude, politics, hair color, automobile, reading list, artistic taste, and fashion sense, as well as the wrong jewelry and religion.

I stared at my husband that night, but really I should have run for the hills, back to Spain. I should have weighed these simple facts: his family is insane and Andalusia is nice that time of year.

I look around the waiting room and notice my husband zoning, in that sort of trance his father used to enter. He told me a couple of days ago that he wished I didn't hate going to his mother's so much. A more appropriate wish would be this: I wish my mother wasn't such a bitch to my wife. I told him that his mother's attitude toward me is not the worst part. The thing I hate most is that he becomes a different person around her, a watered-down, ridiculously conservative version of himself, and not the man I married.

The sad, sad truth is that every time I see my husband with his mother I feel myself loving him less. I worry that it will take me too long to pull that lost love back. I remember my lover and think maybe I missed the clues. Maybe in his own saucer-eyed way, he would have come to love me alone and enough.

One of the Marys laughed when she met me. She found me to be *a little chubby*, I learned later. My original thoughts about them weren't any kinder. I thought, Life is a gift, and there's simply no excuse to travel though it being so dull.

When I tell my father that my mother-in-law hates me, he says he can't believe it. Who wouldn't absolutely love you? he says. I consider giving him a list of the people who didn't absolutely love me, starting with Ms. Gevens, the ballet teacher, letting the list build with a sort of rhythm to my first so-called boyfriend, then the others; a list that reaches a crescendo with my husband's mother and her little ducks. I try to explain how they follow her with indifferent, open beaks. My father and I have always believed the thing that art keeps preaching: there's not enough love in the world.

Women whose fathers are in jail don't want traditional weddings, so my husband and I decided to get married at New York City Hall. His mother stopped speaking to us for two and a half peaceful months. She hated that we hadn't had what she called a proper wedding. This doesn't count, she told my husband, a severe puss on her face. Before I could say a word, he translated. She means it doesn't count as a sacrament; it doesn't qualify with God.

Yeah thanks, I told him. That makes the comment so much easier to swallow.

We received lovely gifts and tributes from our friends. My lover sent congratulations the old fashioned way—via telegram. My father, with the help of my aunt who is not in jail, sent a beautiful letter to my husband with a family heirloom watch, then a sterling tray inscribed to us with my favorite poem. My husband's relatives said and sent nothing. Everyone had been instructed by his mother: this is not a gift giving occasion.

A doctor and nurse walk into the waiting room, talking and nodding to one another. There is a word to describe their nods. Something like somber, but not as intense as somber. It's an S.A.T. sort of word, the kind of thing I never remember.

Before my marriage, I was not the sort of woman who had problems with other women. Mothers liked me. Some of my ex-boyfriends' moms still send a birthday card, which amuses my husband. Everything amuses my husband. I am generally the grown-up.

Okay, my husband isn't into certain Lana activities anymore, but sometimes during sex he slaps my bum good and wild and hard. He's his true self in that moment, free and energy-filled. Later, he'll apologize for getting so out of control, even though he'd meant it, even though I'd liked it. Once again, his early conditioning will have interfered.

I need to remember Madrid. I need my art.

My husband hasn't seen the things I'm doing in my painting class. The most recent is a portrait of him in ten years. I added gray to his hair, fine lines around his eyes. In the painting, he is finally choking, after all these years, his neck caught in a thick gray umbilical chord.

In Madrid we danced. We saw all of the current and hot DJs—they all hit Madrid in the summer. House music fans are older in Europe. We felt like a couple of eighteen-year-olds and my husband did lots of ecstasy. My mother-in-law would have a heart attack if she knew.

Oh, wait.

Now the doctor says something I can't hear, calls out my husband's family name. The nurse leaves, gives Mary Margaret the something-like-somber nod. The Marys nudge their husbands. The husbands wake and scratch heads in unison. The doctor stares at a chart as all of us stand. I'm seeing this through a fog, through the kind of haze my pill-popping friends describe. But I'm not popping anything. I'm just here, in some gray corner of New Jersey, with this strange family the law has related me to.

It's Christmas and I'm not Christian. It's the hospital and I'm feeling far from hospitable. Take a deep breath, I think to myself. Think of painting. Think of Dad.

I catch myself staring at Mary Constance. The simple touch of a nice-looking handbag could do wonders for her. I try to guess if anyone has ever slapped her, shocked that puss off her face. When my husband told Mary Constance he planned to marry me, she said, *That's cute. The chubby one, right?*

I know I'm supposed to forget that sort of thing on Christmas, especially in the hospital, but those are the things taking up space in my head, replacing better memories, finer places, like Madrid, the visiting room at the jail. I want the S.A.T. words back. I want to call my lover.

My husband squeezes my hand. He does this all the time at home, but never in his mother's presence. His mother's presence changes everything. The doctor adjusts his glasses, clears his throat. He steps closer and looks into my eyes.

Blink, I used to tell my lover. Blink and release me. Everything felt both shocking and familiar then. Those first days in Spain, his hair looked dark and dangerous, and I wanted to move closer, to put my nose in his hair and smell it, but my body could not bear to leave the line of his gaze, his focus. Damn you, I almost said, I'm tired. Just blink.

Okay, my father and I were not afflicted with wanderlust or pride exactly. We suffered from hope. My cousin Brooke joked about giving up work-study at NYU to try it as a call girl. My husband said, Don't breathe a word of that to my mother. Yeah, I said, your mother's reaction is the real problem here—not that we live in a society that glamorizes prostitution.

Somehow I have committed to family of submitters—a group that looks like they stepped out of that ancient TV show, *The Waltons*. I feel surrounded by tight collars and denial. Brooke takes an internship at FOX News and stops calling me. My husband says Brooke reminds him of his brother, the one who's in Vancouver, strange and estranged.

Killer bees keep creeping up on the news. *Isn't she the chubby one?* I can't remember how to say chubby or fat in Spanish. I can't imagine how I got to New Jersey. The distraught traveler, the restless tourist, the runaway—I want to flee again, do it all over. A man with saucer eyes will hate bullfights and love me; another will steal my attention and invite me back home.

Did Lana ever believe she could fit in here? Did she want to whack the Marys?

In my dreams people keep telling me to wake up.

The Marys are practical. There is a Spanish word that doesn't mean practical or loveless exactly, but something in between. *You had to upset her, didn't you?* I tell my husband he should call the estranged brother, but Mary Constance says, No, this isn't the time for that sort of thing.

I imagine the estranged brother speaking new languages, discovering the songs he'd been missing. I picture him with a jawline like my husband's, dressing with bright, stylish man bags, sporting killer tattoos, carrying an extra large purple umbrella in the Pacific Northwestern rains, sucking up all the daring and flair that should have been distributed among the Marys.

My father's jail is nothing like the jails on TV. I don't have to speak to him through glass or on a closed-circuit phone. We sit in the middle of the visiting room on cushioned blue chairs. I tell him how pleased I'd been to learn my husband had all those siblings. I wouldn't be an only child anymore, I thought. I'd have three new sisters. But instead of sisters, I tell him, I have three chicks I can barely tolerate, all with the personality of wooden broom handles.

My father says, Hummm, and rubs his chin.

I want my old world back. I want a father who still lives in a brownstone, my own room full of unfinished canvases, and a just-printed plane ticket for crossing the Atlantic. My husband squeezes my hand. He resembles neither my father nor my previous lovers. It's all a bad trip, an off-tempo mix, a concert gone wrong.

Track 17: Blink and Release Me. DJ Merope with special appearance by Jail Daddy. Global Economy Entertainment in association with Heart Attack Studios.

The doctor takes deep breaths before he begins. Ten, nine, eight, buzzing lights and bees. No matter what the news is, this must be the part of his job that the doctor hates, dealing with the families, especially the insane ones.

My husband was the first man I met who had no desire to save me.

I feel the others looking at me. I feel him not noticing— there is so much that they never notice—and continuing to squeeze my hand. There is a strong wind outside, the kind I loved in Madrid, the kind that blew through the trees to create chimes.

Mary Elizabeth isn't ready to look at the doctor, so she looks at me a little longer. There is a place for people like you, she sneers. It is the largest hint of personality I have ever seen from her. I almost want to like her. Then it hits me.

She's right. It was in the news. There *is* a place for people like me—the correctional facility for women who kill their mothers-in-law. I can't believe I didn't think of this. It's in Connecticut, one of the jails that shares a courtyard with my father's. I stand as tall as I can.

It's all my fault, I yell at Mary and Mary and Mary. Brooke's FOX bosses will no exactly how to spin this: A WOMAN IN NEW JERSEY IS ACCUSED OF NEGLIGENT HOMICIDE WHEN HER MOTHER-IN-LAW FALLS OVER BEFORE CHRISTMAS DINNER. That qualifies as news these days, and the media frenzy will be amazing.

You can't blame yourself, my husband says. But I check his eyes and he's blinking. Yes, I say. I grab his arm, clutch it with both hands. Blame me, I tell him. Now I feel it in my chest. I adore him for thinking he shouldn't let me go, but I can't turn back now. My palms are sweating. I'm longing for those tall steel bars to cling to.

I need to get out of this orange room, away from its relentless buzzing. Seven, six, five. The doctor clears his throat again. It's all my fault, I confess to each of the Marys' husbands. They snap out of their trances long enough to nod. Their heads are submissive little mops, willing to go along with whatever I say. They're going to blame me, I instruct the doctor.

The doctor clears his throat again. Five, four... His words may hold my only chance. Three, two... His words come slowly and I need to listen harder because there are so many of them. They come from his mouth and glow like embers, until finally he says the word *recovery*. Embers turn to ash.

Traffic

Margo scans radio stations. She cannot find anything to listen
to. Everything reminds her or fails to remind her of Nathan.
She looks into other cars, at other drivers with their morning
smiles. They must have CD changers, she thinks. They must have
caffeine. She woke craving Mocha Iced Blended. She'd craved iced
coffee during the first months of her work in Burma, but doesn't
think it's a good idea now, back in Los Angeles, en route to Susan's
office. Susan is one of her best friends, also her dentist.

Margo relaxes as she passes Sepulveda and realizes she will
make it on time. Rays of sun beat into West Los Angeles. Cars rush
into the Wilshire Corridor, blood cells hurrying through veins.

She settles on an oldies station. Neil Diamond. *Desiree*. She
decides she wants to hear this story from Desiree's point of view.
Would Desiree agree that the night was right, the time was wrong?

The light turns green. In days, leaving Nathan's apartment
will hurt like an old song and it will be her fault. Another
light turns to green. In the left turn lane, waiting to pour into
Westwood, Margo recalls Wilshire is a fault line.

She feels it as her Jeep and the cars on each side of her turn—the night with Nathan spinning even further away. She wonders how long it will take for each of the Nathan memories to lose their precision.

Nathan sucks her left nipple. She hopes he'll give the same attention to the right, because it seems that the right is never as hard, that the right can never catch up.

She says I really like—she is careful not to say love—being naked with you. I really like the feeling of being attracted to you. I like the sound of your voice saying my name.

Margo. Be quiet, he says, his voice just above a whisper.

She doesn't want to be quiet. She doesn't want him to be. She wants to be grounded by his questions. She wants to fall in love with the things he asks. Because right now this seems like a dream. He is a hard and hairy dream.

They meet at Lola's, his idea, for dirty martinis, also his idea. She wears leather pants. She has been in tents and trekking gear for months, so these things feel good to her: playing with olives, lingering in lounges, dressing like a babe. They sit at the bar, and he touches the ring on her right hand. Jade from Mandalay, she says. I saw it, and I had to have it. He looks away.

What? she says.

Nothing, he says.

When he turns back to her, she gives him her olives.

He doesn't say Welcome back; he doesn't ask about Burma or what she's doing now that she's home. He only says, Did you catch anything?

Just food poisoning, she says. A weak stomach. I barfed a lot.

Nice, he says, and smiles.

At Lola's, he does not have to tell her there is someone else in his life. Tonight her instincts are green. So to save him the tensions of explaining, Margo says, She must be wonderful, this woman who has captured your imagination.

His mouth opens, stunned. Yes, he says. Margo rolls the stem of her glass in her fingers. He fidgets, so Margo keeps talking. What are the things you love about her? she asks, then wishes she hadn't. She has gone too personal too soon; she has gone too far.

He clears his throat. I love so many things about her, he says. I love her schedule.

Her schedule?

Yeah, she's an actress.

Margo throws back the rest of a martini. She knows it's the jealousy seeping in, or maybe the gin soaking in, but her fingertips start to burn.

She cannot believe he said actress. He is a music man. Shouldn't he fall in love with a choreographer or conductor? An oboe or French horn? She can live with the idea of envying oboe players. How many can there be? But she hates the idea of envying actresses. There are thousands in Los Angeles alone.

Her toes start to burn as well. They're not truly burning, she knows, but yearning. For Burmese soil. In Burma, there is said to be no envy. It's not a very Buddhist notion.

Are you and your actress love—she wants to ask, selfishly, about monogamy—exclusive?

I'd like to be, he says.

Margo orders a new martini.

Are you sure that's a good idea? Nathan asks. But Margo ignores his question and he orders one too.

She wants to know some little thing about him, a detail she didn't before. Something about him alone, not the actress. But he doesn't say a word. He pulls his piccolo from his jacket pocket and puts it to his lips. He is a piccolo player, but she knew that already.

So he plays his piccolo during lulls in conversation. The bartender laughs and people stare. *I thought about you a lot,* she says. He keeps playing and shrugs his shoulders, as if this is the most normal thing he has ever heard, as if women on the other side of Earth think about him all the time. In Burma, she thinks, those tense, creaking, high-pitched sounds come from words.

In Amarapura couples drink juice made from sugarcane. *Ka`*, they say, to suggest a dance. Monks step toward foreigners and say, in their most careful English, *Yes, so glad you arrive here.*

Hours later, Margo sinks back into his bed, on top of blankets, propped on her elbows. Nathan pushes at her clothes and licks her stomach. He runs his nose along her ribs. By the time they pull clothes off, the coarseness of his blankets have left burns on her elbows.

He dims the lights, leaving the room gray. Her chest and stomach ache with wanting. They lie on their sides, he puts his forehead against hers, closes his eyes. He says: *You do understand that this can only be tonight, don't you?*

It is already more than tonight, she wants to say. *It is last year and the 3.5 million times I thought of you on the Myanmar peninsula.*

He turns from her. Margo presses her chest against his back, rests her chin on his shoulder, looks over him as he reaches from the bed, fumbles through the bottom drawer of his nightstand, the storage place for his condoms. Too much olive, she thinks. Too many martinis.

On top of the nightstand rests a card from his nephew. *For Nat.* In Burma, a nat is a spirit, with power to protect or harm. Performers invite nats to possess and protect their medium, but sometimes nats miss; they possess and harm people instead.

There's so much to say, she says. This is when he lingers on her left nipple.

And so little, he says. She is grabbing his ass.

You want me to shut up, she says. Her hands are everywhere now, moving without direction from her brain. Her hands want to warm, keep, and ruin him.

Yes, he says. Finally he moves to the right nipple. But it will never catch up. She knows. Her hands slow. She runs her lips through the cave of his neck, hoping her lips, like her hands, will memorize his shape and form. His ears smell like soap. His neck smells like gin.

She reaches below his waist, ignores his penis for a moment, reaches for his testicles. There are two of them, thank God, two large and perfect balls. She feared that she'd failed to notice the first time, that there would be only one, and he would think that in only a year she had forgotten his details. He tangles his fingers in her hair. She worries that she will ruin everything by saying by wrong thing, by reaching for something that was never there.

You're so beautiful, she says.

No more talking, he says. You have a darling ass, he says. Heart-shaped, he adds. You talk too much, he says. You have no idea how fucked up I am, he says.

I don't want to know, she laughs, but the second she says it, realizes she does. It's possible she loves his faults even before he reveals them.

I think I was meant to be with you.

Sush, he says. That's the alcohol talking.

He smiles. She feels the shape of his smile on her right breast. Catch up, she thinks. *Catch up.* There are endless moments of touching and clutching until he is on top, his penis inside her. She keeps one hand on his two testicles. He kisses her hard, but it is a kiss she cannot decipher. He may want her quiet; he may want her breath.

She misses him before he comes. She misses him before she's gone.

Margo arrives back at her apartment at quarter to eight in the morning. She replays and replays the night in her aching head. She should shower, get out of last night's clothes, but feels exhausted from recollections. Her voicemail is full of messages from her girlfriends.

They're at an after-hours club where Angie's working. Angie is the so-called bad girl of the group. Margo became an anthropologist, Lena a historical preservationist, and Susan a dentist, but Angie left school to dance and sew. By night, she shimmies, humps, and poses atop a six-foot stage while wearing a vinyl catsuit. By day, she sews one-of-a-kind sleep masks for a boutique at Fred Segal. She is the sort of person who always knows what to say. Margo feels glad to know that while she was in Burma none of them lost the ability to stay out all night.

Hey, Lena says. We're celebrating your return without you.

Where are you exactly? Margo says. She manages to laugh.

Sin-a-matic at Ultra Suede, Lena says. It ends at nine.

It is a Los Angeles thing. A moving nightclub within a stationary one, people dancing through the night. Hey, come for the last hour, Lena says. We'll dance for a while, grab breakfast. We'll get your mind off Whoever-He-Is.

That won't be easy, Margo says. Despite her best efforts, her voice cracks.

For a moment Margo considers going. A club with Sin in the name would have uninhibited gyrating men—not unavailable men playing piccolos. She misses her friends. She likes the idea of wearing leather to Ultra Suede. She sinks into her sofa and kicks her shoes off.

She hears Lena whispering at Susan. *Hey, she sounds bad.* They're worried.

Susan gets on the line and says Mar, we'll get Angie and call you back. I'm not sure the club will cheer you up. It's a little depressing, I think—just human traffic.

When they call Margo from Lena's car at nine, she tells them the basics, not the details. He is not her secret to tell, but he isn't her secret to keep either. Lena says, She mistook him for the one. Angie says, Yes, she has mistaken him for home.

Lena and Angie have long-time boyfriends. Susan married an orthodontist.

Lena and Angie keep saying, Are you sure you're okay? They make antidote jokes. You need Alanis, they say, or Simone de Beauvior. Susan obsesses on oral hygiene. You're sure his tongue was red? she asks. Because if his tongue was greenish, you shouldn't have kissed him at all.

His tongue was red, Margo says. He is a musician, and he has two balls.

Yes, Sweetie, Angie sighs, that's usually the way it works.

In Los Angeles, copper wire loops are embedded into every lane on each freeway and major artery. There are more than 20,000 loops working at a time, transmitting data over phone lines and through satellites to a center where traffic patterns are studied.

Margo thinks of this now, as she watches in her rearview mirror cars coming from the 405 Freeway. Somewhere out there, Nathan's car may be driving over a copper loop, sending data to an office far away from here, data that someone will trust.

The first time she spent the night with Nathan, he kissed her goodnight and clung to her in his sleep. In the morning she woke with a start, squinted at the clock. He pulled her close and said, It's so early. Please don't go.

The next day she had to leave for Burma.

The second and last time with Nathan, after martinis at Lola's, was one year and 30,000 air miles later. They drank too much. She had to try to keep any idea of love out of it. They fucked; he patted her ass three times and rolled to the opposite edge of the bed. In the dark of morning Nathan woke first, pulled Margo's clothes from the floor, tossed them to her, then watched her untangle the bra from the jacket and the jacket from the camisole. He started his goodbye before her shoes were on.

She wanted to say What? No coffee this time? No *please stay*. No eggs benedict? Guilt made his eyes hard. She realized then the difference between a brief love affair and a one-night stand. With the love affair you get hollandaise.

Nathan had walked into Lola's that night with his hair combed back, his brilliant smile. He wore a long leather jacket with a deep pocket that held the piccolo. He put his hands on her face and kissed her forehead. Her heart rushed to her ankles and back. Her neck tingled. She fingered the jade on her ring. One of the Burmese words for jade means, literally, a strange lump of time. Margo recalled the way the two of them laid on their sides one year ago, looking to each other, half of each face hidden in the pillow.

Margo watches the light, scratches her neck, waits for a green arrow. She remembers an English-speaking man who drove her in Yangon. Human behind wheel, he said, road unstable. Yes, she said, and they laughed. In Burma, he hadn't relied on special copper wires to know it.

She had worked hard to get to Burma; Botswana and Java before that. She likes the process of her work, the way she can expand, then focus; study a new place, anticipate it. Los Angeles is the contrast to every place she knows. She watches women waiting to board the Wilshire bus, a stream of men stepping off and rushing past them. The city spills out around her.

The very first time she saw Nathan—International Day at Crossroads School—she felt her stomach in her knees. She had been invited to give a presentation on the cultures of Indonesia. Nathan, a Crossroads alum, had been the guest of his eleven-year-old nephew. Nathan and Margo never spoke that day. He stared and she noticed. The nephew, bolder than Nathan, thanked her at the end of her talk and asked if she had a boyfriend.

A month and three days later Nathan and Margo reached for the same copy of *The Best American Essays* at Midnight Special Bookstore. There is a God, Margo thought. What are the chances, in a metropolitan area of nine million people, they'd stop into the same bookstore on the same night; in a collection of more than 100,000 books, they'd reach for the very same one?

They laughed at their awkwardness, but after the laughter it felt like they'd known one another for years. They leaned against bookshelves and read to each other. They read of Mozart and blood, gemstones and beans. His voice was a song.

Her fingers trembled when she felt nervous. She noticed, as he turned pages, that his did too. She knew it then: good or bad, this could only end in his bedroom.

In a sleep tent in Burma, Margo would see in her mind all of the things they would do together. Outdoor concerts at the Hollywood Bowl, gallery openings at Bergamont Station, hikes in the Santa Monica Mountains. She imagined the way he would nudge her during the funny part in a movie, the way he would put her face in his hands when he kissed her hello. Anthropology was a science that allowed for imagination.

She imagined and imagined and imagined.

The day she arrived home she noticed two new lanes on the Long Beach Freeway. Still, traffic jammed. She knew what this meant. Commuters' needs had outraced engineers' dreams. It was only in my head, she thought. I experienced the relationship on a continuous reel in my brain.

There is so much to say, she had said to Nathan when

she returned. It wasn't the alcohol talking. She wanted him to know that without meaning to he had fascinated her more than Yangon's pagodas and temples or Pindaya Caves. He'd taken her attention in Burma, before the bustle of morning markets, the wondrous sea turtles, the tallest banana trees.

And so little, he had said.

In an essay, Somerset Maugham wrote that Burma's beauty batters you, stuns you, leaves you breathless. He warned friends to guard against its intensity by saying to themselves that it couldn't have been real. Margo hadn't had the chance to say that to Nathan.

Westwood traffic is worse than usual. The Jetta in front of Margo's Jeep screeches to a stop. Dozens of sport-shorted students rush through the crosswalk on Gayley Avenue.

There I was bound by the sweet crashing sound...

They jump into L.A. Fitness, dressed for TaeBo.

Margo has missed most of the TaeBo craze but thinks she might benefit from a kick or two. She should have left Lola's alone, she thinks. It is her own fault she feels this way. One cannot live in Los Angeles without learning faults: breaks in rock formation, defects caused by imperfect connections. She knew about the actress and she went home with him anyway.

Margo moves into the turn lane. *So I tossed and I turned while the thought of it burned up and down my mind.* She doesn't remember Desiree lasting so long.

She feels thankful for Susan.

Susan will hug Margo in front of the reception desk, squeeze her hand, compliment her dress. But Margo wonders if the dress makes her look a little too flower child, a little too wounded. Susan—a perfect blend of energy and grace, her blonde hair pulled back, her lab coat falling softly across her body—would know better than to spend a year thinking about a piccolo man. Women and men fall for Susan every day. If she's not drilling their teeth.

Another crosswalk. This time she waits for three men in suits gripping Starbucks cups. She misses the pedestrian crowds of Burma, the Pathein men with fine bamboo umbrellas. She is stuck at the crosswalk as more men dart out of Starbucks and into the street.

Margo thinks of bacteria. She thinks her mouth a cave for the sediment of everything that nourishes her. It seems impossible that only last week the people around her wore grass sandals and *longyis*. There must be microscopic parts of Nathan that couldn't be forced from her mouth, she thinks. Her toothbrush and all the rinses in the world might not do the job, so Susan's hygienist will scrape it away.

She pulls into the parking garage, up the spiral ramp, and tandems her Jeep with Susan's car. In Burma, there are no expressways, spillbacks, rotaries, or interchanges. There are few bottlenecks. Signs forbid horns, and roads might wash away. Everything is red. Not stoplight red, but an aged, earthy, pimento red. Sweet Desiree red. Outside Yangon—she loves the sound of this word, *Yangon*—orchid trees burst with irregular scarlet flowers.

Susan's office overlooks the UCLA campus. From the top of the parking garage Margo can see the roof of Royce Hall. Performing artists, Margo thinks. Poetry, polyphonies, piccolos. She must take the garage elevator to the lobby, the lobby elevator to the office. I could have stayed in Burma, she thinks. I could have remained among monks.

From the first lobby she calls for the second elevator. Do not use during earthquake or fire, a warning plate says. Violators will be subject to fines.

Absurdity, lust, shaking beds, she thinks.

Hot canyons, obstructions, gridlock.

A security guard nods in her direction. Sunlight bathes the floor around him. Elevator takes a bit, he says. Margo nods back.

She recalls the way Nathan felt and kissed each of her hipbones, the way he positioned himself above her. Yet he had not assumed a relationship with Margo. That was the sorrow of it. She had experienced a romance; for Nathan it was simply a date.

A bell sounds for the elevator but it takes several moments for the doors to open. She steps inside, smells the sting of cinnamon another passenger's perfume has left behind. She breathes it in. She missed basic lessons in Burma, she thinks. The Buddhist's eightfold path, the eight spokes on a wheel. In the east, people do not cling. In the east, they let go. She is from the west, so she hung on. She hangs.

Margo recalls that bronze Buddhas crafted in Mandalay Style have eyes staring straight ahead, hands hovering over their legs rather than resting upon them. She knows she will have to fight to forget Nathan. She knows now, that if there had been one ball, she would have touched it, held it, stroked it, kissed it, and pushed from her mind any thought of a missing partner.

Three Naked Men

The first naked man was Rocco, a neighborhood legend, on the day of my husband's funeral. Rocco was known for walking his dog naked every spring and summer morning, but had the reasonably good sense to do this at 4 a.m., while most of the community slept. I'd never seen him, but my neighbor Bea swore it was true. En route to her 6 a.m. business flights, she'd see Rocco walking up Oakview, his Jack Russell on a leash, his own penis bopping in front of him. Bea said that Kathleen, an insomniac down the block, watched him though her bay window and had taken to greeting him as he passed. Bea said that when winter came, Kathleen was really going to miss him.

That morning, I sat in the window in our study and stared out to the empty street. I'd stared myself into such a trance that I might not have seen Rocco walk by at all. But he had something in his hand, a lavender envelope. It must have been later than usual for Rocco. The sun rose through the trees, made faint stripes of light on the street. Rocco stopped at our mailbox, tucked the envelope inside. He looked across our yard toward our front door, dropped his head for a moment, and when the Jack Russell got impatient, Rocco looked up and continued on.

It was one of those strange Illinois mornings when the sun shines hard and the humidity disappears for a few hours, leaving the grass crisp and cold. Eventually I heard Caitlin's alarm go off in her room, the shower start in her bathroom. She'd set her alarm even though she hadn't slept either. I should have been in the shower by that time too. I'm not sure what I was waiting for exactly, the sound of my husband gargling his mouthwash, a phone call that said it had all been a big mistake. When the phone did ring, it was the funeral home director saying the limousine would be in front of our house in an hour.

We live in the kind of town where everyone has something to say, or thinks they have to say something. It makes me miss the city, the anonymity Caitlin never knew. My husband and I moved here sixteen years ago, before she was born.

In the weeks after his death, people placed their hands on Caitlin's shoulder at the drug store, yogurt shop, the dry cleaner's, saying they knew her father. Caitlin glared.

She knew she was supposed to say something, to thank them for something, for nothing, for saying whatever they'd said. But it just seemed stupid, she told her grandmother, my mother, to act like this stranger knew about her loss, to feel hostage to some sort of expected dialogue. What she wanted to say was, Big fucking deal, my dad was a popular guy and everyone thinks they knew him.

I know what I'm supposed to say, she'd complained to me later. I just don't want to say it.

When my husband and I were newlyweds in the city, we saw a short film where a young man arrived in heaven and had forgotten his wife's name. He remembered everything else about her—her smell, the ease with which she ran a comb through her hair, her favorite kind of cookie—but her name escaped him. He walked across the blue cloud-lined streets of heaven trying to figure it out. Amber, he said. Buffy, Constance, Malinda, Natalie, Quinn, Rose, Samara? Grace? Pia? And he went on and on like that until he collapsed in exhaustion at the end of the road.

So what do you think her name was? my husband wanted to know at the end.

I think the point of the film is that it doesn't matter what her name was.

He nodded his head.

Her name was Lilly, my husband said when we'd left the theater.

The man in heaven said Lilly three times. Each of the other names occurred only once. He remembered; he just got confused.

Caitlin picked at the edges of her toast every morning, hardly ate breakfast. Bea said all the girls were doing that, that it was more about her age than her grief.

If you think you would like to go to counseling, I told Caitlin, we'll go.

She ignored me, sat down at the table, reached for a magazine she'd left there, maybe weeks ago. Eat something, I told her. And I hated that I said it the minute I said it, because I sounded so much like my own mother. My mother thought that putting a slab of pie in front of someone was generally the best answer to their problems.

I'm serious about the counseling, I said. I don't want to end up like the Simonoffs.

I'd just met Marina Simonoff when her husband was killed in a freeway collision. Her family was a portrait of strength in those days, fifteen years ago. All these years later, they looked pale and wrecked, leaving their jobs to spend months at a time in New Mexico, at spas with famous shrinks in residence.

My daughter's ears turned red. That's what you're worried about? she screamed.

When it happened to us, Marina was one of the first people here. She told Caitlin and me, Don't go numb. Try to remember everything.

Caitlin threw her magazine down and pushed hard away from the table.

That's what concerns you? That we'll be like the Simonoffs?

Before I could answer, she had gone. Her bedroom door slammed closed.

Caitlin watered the garden while I swept the patio. Her friends had stayed late the night before, watching DVDs and drinking whiskey sours with little whisky—whatever someone had snuck away from their parent's bottle at home, which couldn't have been too much. My husband's brother planned to drive out that day for my husband's sweaters—the ones Caitlin hadn't sequestered for herself.

People might think you're a little crazy, Caitlin said, parting with Dad's stuff so soon.

It's not everything, Caitlin. It's just the sweaters. And they'll say I'm crazy if I part with things too late, so what difference does it make?

Caitlin yawned and left the hose in one place too long, making puddles.

I hate it here, she said.

She meant this town. She meant this place without her father.

Actually, she said, perking up, what's the movie where the crazy widow burns everything? She runs around the yard in a lace nightgown, throwing things into a fire pit.

She said it like it was a good idea.

I think this neighborhood got its dose of crazy fire last summer, I said, sweeping harder.

Caitlin sighed, went back to making puddles.

Last June, Bea left her husband for two months. On week three he built a fire and burned all of her clothes. Everything: sandals, Spanx, ponytail holders, her gym bag. Burt's fire made the newspaper's police log. Bea is still pissed about it.

For fuck's sake, there was Escada in there, she said later. Anyway, Burt knew there was an excellent chance I was coming back.

She hates the word dead. My daughter hates the words crash, accident, and remains. Can't we just say he passed? she wanted to know.

Passed what? I thought. Passed into what? It was more accurate to say he was killed. Also more painful.

Passed is fine, I assured her. I imagined Caitlin years from then, lying on a secondhand sofa with a boyfriend both wrong and right for her because he was nothing like her father. She would cry during the late news, and neither would pinpoint exactly the single phrase that brought her tears: the victims' families.

The coroner in our town was old school, so my husband's identity was confirmed through dental records. My father went to our dentist's office to get the file. When he returned, he left the folder sitting on the desk in the study. When the coroner's messenger arrived the folder was gone. I raced through the house, looking on every surface, in every drawer, until Caitlin pulled the folder out of its hiding place in the kitchen cabinet.

What's it doing there? my father wanted to know.

So many people are here, Caitlin gasped, folding her arms.

Her cheeks looked stained; her bangs hung in her face. She had to concentrate to keep her voice from cracking. What if someone needs to use your office phone? Do you have any idea how upsetting it would be for them to see his dental records just sitting out?

The three of us stared at each other, stone-faced, uncomprehending.

Bright trays had appeared on my kitchen counter. Fruit displays, wheels of summer salami, rows of crackers with spreads and cheeses, foil-wrapped casseroles and lasagnas, pickled eggs, no-bake cakes, every kind of cookie imaginable, plus honey-baked hams.

Caitlin was right, the people kept coming, my mother greeting friends and relatives at the front door, my father greeting neighbors at the back. They were all there: a tribe made of my husband's clients and colleagues from Detroit, Milwaukee, and St. Louis; every member of Caitlin's soccer team, dance class, and Spanish club, most with their parents; our first, second, and third cousins; Great Aunt Judy, who'd knitted things for our very first anniversary; my husband's college friends, their wives, girlfriends, or boyfriends; old roommates; friends from the city that we hadn't seen since Caitlin was a baby; my husband's basketball friends; people who served with him on the boards of the community center and historical society; the tailor; the accountant; an old friend who had designed the cake for our wedding; Caitlin's teachers; parents from her schools; my parent's friends and neighbors; the woman who owned our favorite restaurant; my boss and her children, even her ex-husband; our old landlord; the handyman; the hairdresser; Caitlin's first babysitter and swim instructor; friends we'd made at parties, jogging, and playing cards.

The second naked man was on the side of Garfield Road.

Caitlin and I were on the way to the airport, getting away,

spending the end of summer in a rental house in southwestern France. Caitlin campaigned against the trip at first; everyone in my life advised against it. It's crazy, my parents said. You need to be here; you need your friends; you shouldn't be spending money. But I didn't need to be anywhere, I could afford the trip, and my friends were my friends no matter how many miles occurred between us. Caitlin had her summer break from school, I'd taken a leave of absence from work anyway, and the rental was a steal.

I'm just not sure this is right for Caitlin, my mother kept saying.

Caitlin could do worse than Sarlat-la-Canéda, I assured her.

It was dark that night—my headlights caught him only for a moment, standing between the road and the ditch, still as a statue, staring into the night. Caitlin sat in the passenger seat, quiet and tall, arms folded as usual. At the naked man, she lurched forward, turned her head as we passed, insisted we should stop.

Caitlin, we're not stopping for a naked man on Garfield road.

He could be in trouble, she said.

He could be dangerous, I said.

He probably needs help. He may have been beaten, or robbed, or worse. And we just whizzed by in our nice car like we don't have a care in the world.

I have many cares, I informed her. And I'm not missing my plane for a naked, insane man standing near a ditch.

She lowered her eyelids, narrowed her gaze—a look I'd come to know as, Mom, you're the one who's insane.

This is just like you, she said.

What is just like me?

Fearing people who need nothing more from you than a little help. Like when we're in Chicago and you go out of your way to avoid homeless people on the street. I mean, do you really think ignoring them is the answer? All they want is a meal or a drink or some fucking pocket change.

Watch your mouth, I told her.

Whatever, she said. When you see in the news that some destitute man died alone in the ditch, that dozens of cars must have driven by, but no one stopped—

That's enough, Caitlin.

We'd both had enough, I thought. She slouched into her seat, stared out the window.

Bea had agreed to keep an eye on the house. I stopped the papers and the mail. Sympathy cards still came to the house, and for a while the true meaning of them had escaped me. Maybe I feared being home when they stopped coming for good, those lovely and well-meant cards that kept recalling the fact that I would never see my husband again. Except the Christian cards, which kept insisting that I would if I had faith.

Several cards, with purple flowers on their flaps and pastel envelopes, let me think instead of my grandmother and the way she used to put perfume in her hair. I may not have faith, I thought, but I'll have France.

Your father loved Southwestern France, I said to Caitlin then.

She answered me by mumbling in French, which was impressive, even if I couldn't hear what she had said. She was angry with me also for leaving my wedding ring at home.

Before the plane reached the skies over the edge of the Atlantic that night, Caitlin had started writing to friends at home, boys she called Jacko and Soup.

Dad would have kept his ring on, she told me later, and I wondered how she could possibly know such a thing.

The third naked man hid in the trees along the Dordogne River.

Caitlin and I woke early that day, drove from our house near Sarlat to the water for our *excursion en canoe*. The skies were slightly cloudy, and for a moment I considered postponing and going to see the cave paintings instead. Caitlin had been sleepy, but perked up right away when the woman working the rental area showed us a bright red canoe and several others. I like the red, Caitlin decided.

Oui, pour l'avenirs brilliants, the woman told us.

As we set out, I started telling Caitlin how to hold the oar, but she rolled her eyes and said she knew. I didn't remember us ever canoeing.

They call this the Land of 1001 Chateaux, I said.

You told me that before, she said, but without her usual sass. Trees kept the edges of the river shaded, so we decided to stay right in the warmth of the center.

Dad and I took a canoe across some inland lake in Michigan the year I was a Brownie and we went to father-daughter camp. Caitlin looked up and down the river as she said it, searching something that wasn't there.

Dad was really good at it, and the rowboat too, she said. And making the fire.

I had been slow to understand that Caitlin knew many things about her father I did not; that they belonged to each other in the way of daughters and fathers, a way they would never belong to me. Maybe my mom was right to say that this trip wasn't for Caitlin. Perhaps I had been selfish to insist on the Dordogne Valley, a place where I had traveled with her father before she was born, when we were young, just starting in our careers and our marriage, and I hadn't had to share him with so many people. The world has made me the guardian of his legacy, yet Caitlin shares his genes. It is a legacy that belongs to her.

Earth to Mom, Caitlin called. She was doing an excellent job with the oar.

I remembered Caitlin running in the door, seven years old, her nose peeling and her face as brown as her Brownie beanie. Before I could lecture my husband about sunblock, she screamed, Mom, we had the best time!

Really? I looked to my husband. He nodded, tired and happy. At first he hadn't wanted to go. He had never been camping. He joked that he didn't work his ass off all week to pretend at homelessness on the weekends. But he'd had a great time too, and they couldn't stop laughing about how they lost a relay race and had to clean dishes for the entire camp.

Past this stretch of forest, I tell her, I think we'll get a good view of the village.

Caitlin saw him first, the naked man stepping out from behind the trees, waving to us. This one wanted to be seen.

Don't wave back, she warned. I have a bad vibe about this one.

As we negotiated the water and glided past, the naked man stood in his patch of trees, posing in our direction. He put the palm of one hand on a tree trunk, adjusted his pose slightly as our speed increased, then he disappeared.

It's creepy, the way he's standing, Caitlin said. Something's not right.

We sat tall, suddenly sharpened, attuned to the world around us. We heard the brush of the water, birds singing and calling. My husband and I must have heard thousands of different sounds when we traveled. Could it have been hundreds of thousands? Humans should have a keener sense of hearing, I thought. We should be able to remember the quality of every waterway, every voice.

In the distance I heard the hum of an engine.

Can that be a car? Caitlin said.

I looked back to the trees near the place the naked man had been. The sun came brighter and Caitlin squinted. I shaded my eyes with my hands and saw that beyond the trees, a little white car sped along a dirt path.

He was driving to the next bend, to expose himself again.

The Challenge of
Acting Normal

D awn leaves his apartment building with her bra stuffed
in her purse. As she steps toward a taxi, she looks at her
reflection in the half-open passenger window. The driver
introduces herself as Charlene, says the last customer spilled his
drink all over the back, invites Dawn to sit up front. Charlene
has hair the color of butter, vanilla, and brown sugar, and a voice
like gravel. She pulls a cassette from a bag on the floor, shoves
it into the tape deck. I love this heavy 80s shit, Charlene says.

Here I am... The song is *Rock You Like a Hurricane*. Dawn
remembers it as one the so-called bad boys listened to in junior
high. Dawn squints into the sunlight. Her eyes are smudged with
last night's make-up. She tastes his toothpaste in her mouth. She
has used his toothbrush.

Maybe the music, or her smudged eyes, bring the word
slut to her mind. I look like a slut, she thinks to herself. She
grins without meaning to. As metal blares through a speaker
mounted in the back of the cab, Dawn makes a mental inventory
of the moment.

She has left his apartment in last night's dress and cardigan, her bra in her purse.

She feels thankful that they woke together, that the morning was not awkward.

She is twenty-six years old.

She is average, but feeling giddy and gorgeous, even with smudged mascara.

She is 970 miles from home.

She is a flight attendant, but not the sort who has a man in every hub city.

She is staying with her friend Ally, who is generous with keys, not questions.

She is freshly fucked—they did it five times and all over the apartment, in fact.

As fate would have it, she's listening to The Scorpions.

And hard as she tries, as exciting as it would be, she cannot feel like a slut.

I am a slut, she whispers. She gives the word another chance, tries it on again, but it won't hold. And Charlene, if she had heard Dawn's whisper over The Scorpions, would never believe it, even with Dawn's crumpled dress and whisker-burned cheeks and neck. Dawn's look, even today, is that of a responsible woman blossomed from a reasonably well-educated girl.

It is so damned annoying, she thinks, to have spent so much of twenty-six years meeting expectations, failing to stir things up. She wants to remain the woman she is at this very moment—the one who somehow knows all the words to *Rock You Like a Hurricane*, who has the slightest tingle of spermicide remaining inside her.

When Dawn pays Charlene, she thanks her for the song.

As Dawn steps into Ally's shower, she feels steam against her face and thinks that last night was the reason she was put on Earth. She knows she's taking herself too seriously, that she'll laugh at herself for this later. Isn't that what critics say about

The Scorpions—that they took themselves way too seriously?

Here I am.

Ally's shower always holds some elegant surprise. This time it is a peach perfumed soap in the shape of a diaphragm. Dawn touches her nipples, still hard somehow, as if they'd had his tongue on them only moments ago. She thinks of flying home now, ending the story before craving the phone call that might continue it.

In her mind she has already labeled it a story, decided how she might start it for Ally.

When he finally kisses her... It was in an elevator and they were going up. When he moved toward her, she noticed his eyes, watery red from smoke, booze, and wanting. She cannot remember the time between the elevator and his apartment door.

When he finally kisses her... It was in an elevator, and because she'd nearly given up on that kiss ever coming, it took her by surprise

When he finally kisses her, it is in an elevator and they are going up. Her chest hurts with the way she craves him. She wants her dress to explode.

For the rest of today she will see him in her mind. A feeling knots together in her stomach. The water feels colder. Her friends insist this kind of thing is no big deal, so why is her world changed?

Slut, slut, slut, she sings to the showerhead, but the word still doesn't belong to her. Charlene has crossed town by now. Today, hanging out with Ally, Dawn will try to act normal. She stands in cool water, shaking it off, breathing it in, becoming stranger.

An Interrogation at the Prison of Ex-Girlfriends

We were bound but not gagged; the wife wanted us to talk. Her assistant had done the dirty work—jumped us in the street, knocked us out, transported us to wherever the hell we were, tied us tight to wooden chairs. It was my day off. I had been walking the Highline. I heard footsteps behind me, turned, and everything went black.

Stop staring, the assistant barked. She was big and butch, safe for the wife to have around, I thought. She slapped her whip in my direction. The wife reached into her cardigan pocket and pulled out some pills. She shoved them in her mouth and gulped them down without water.

He had never described the wife correctly and now I hated him for it. When we were together he had tried to say that he had never been in love with her, that they married because he was the proper age to start a family and she had the right attributes.

That sounds so cold, I told him.

Does it? he asked, even though he knew it did.

She was pretty in a classic way, an Upper East Side way—

that much was predictable. She had perfect bone structure and big brown eyes. They looked beautifully misplaced, like they should appear on a little girl. If I hadn't been her prisoner, I might have liked her.

I heard some of the other women straining, struggling with their ropes. Why wasn't I fighting? My head was throbbing and I could feel swelling on my face. Tied up with two black eyes—while coming to I must have decided I deserved it.

Do things make more or less sense when you are tied up? I looked at the wife. Or when you commissioned the tying?

The room was slightly dark; all cement, grey and dusk-like. Wooden crates created walls on each side of us. God only knew what was in them.

It was easy to imagine him falling in love with the wife, impossible to imagine that she would not have had a life without him, which was one of the things he always said. To the contrary, she may have felt cheated with him, even before his cheating.

He said he had misbehaved even when they were dating, engaged. Back then he was the kind of schmuck who hadn't really known how to be happy, he said. It was a statement that meant little to me at the time because I didn't believe in happiness. Not in a dark way, but in a practical way. What can happiness possibly mean when it is supposed to support so many different things for so many people?

So yes, like the other women tied up in that room, I hadn't backed off when I learned he was married. In my defenses to my friends I used to point out that he was separated, or so he said. At the time I denied how married separated people actually are. Separated people are trying to hold it together, which takes a certain effort and dedication—ironically, a kind of loyalty.

I had spent quite a bit of time in therapy wondering how I could have been such a shit. Tied to that chair, I wondered how he could have been such a shit, how he risked never seeing her eyes again. If this had happened when we were together I would have told him, Your biggest problem right now is that I sort of like her. Certainly undertaking a group abduction required more verve than I had ever imagined from a wife. If she had been my friend and not my abductor, I might have cheered her on.

He had lied incessantly but petals from the endless array of flower bouquets he sent never failed at the straight-up truth. *He loved me not.*

Taking the whip from the assistant, the wife studied each one of us. I wiggled in my chair as she stared, felt guilty that she was failing to scare me. Her whip looked less like a weapon to me than a prop from a fetish party. This was the sort of thing I could have never said to him—he was more conservative, and likely had never even heard of a fetish party.

He had laughed once at a nightclub invitation he saw on top of my mail. MIDNIGHT SPANKING HOUR; FOAM FEST TO FOLLOW. I never went to those things, but he thought my life must be somewhat ridiculous for my name to appear on the mailing list in the first place.

The wife's assistant followed behind her trying to keep the long handled ax steady on her shoulder. I heard static in the distance, like voices from an old radio.

Fighting the ropes started to seem like a good idea. Clearly the butch assistant could go rogue at any moment. When I first came to, the assistant had checked the tightness of my ropes and said, Cute notes, Fantasy You. And of course, I cringed. I would have liked to have forgotten that part; to not have known what she meant.

When we were together, he had called from a business trip late one night. We were about to say naughty things on the phone when my roommate burst in, crying and needing to talk. There was no acceptable excuse to send her away and stay on the phone, so I whispered, Why don't you continue with Fantasy Me tonight, and I'll catch up with Fantasy You in the morning. I thought it was cute at the time, along with the string of now regrettable Fantasy You and Fantasy Me emails. The wife had seen them. Of course she had.

I looked around the room for the hundredth time. There were probably twenty of us, maybe less than one would have expected considering his energy level and determination—or was that sexual addiction? I'd never expected to be in the same room with any of them, but he was a talker, so I felt like I knew them. I looked for the bruised versions of the dermatologist, the florist, the music producer, the waitress. That was only a fifth of them. Whoever they were around me, they were pissed off, thin, and gently pretty—not a huge surprise. It would have been better for the wife if we looked like seductresses. He did the seducing.

I had no idea where we were, but I could still hear radio static. It may have been my imagination, but I thought I could make out NPR on the other side of the crate wall. There was something comforting about being close to NPR.

We might be safe for a moment, I reasoned, until she accepted the tragedy of it. That holding us there, whatever information we might share, would not change a thing.

I looked for the girlfriend after me, the Israeli dancer, the one he thought he might marry, or so he confessed one gloomy day during a chance post-relationship Starbucks run-in— ignoring for a moment the fact that actually he was married.

She was supposed to have puffed out, over-done lips. If the wife knew about the rest of us surely she knew about Lips. Lips must be sitting behind me, out of view. My friend Duff, a bartender at the Shoreham, had seen them together at the hotel and promised me she was a troll. As if that helped. Actually, I informed him, big lips, long arms, whatever—I preferred to be replaced by a goddess. Presumably Lips and I were both here, two years later, knocked down and tied up by the wife.

The ropes burned hard into my wrists and ankles. I tried to tell myself it hurt slightly less than laser hair removal until there was no denying that it hurt more.

I remembered how he would hold my hands to his face and say, Look baby, I shaved for you. I would say, Whatever, my bikini line has endured expensive and excruciating laser procedures for you.

It was pathetic but looking at his other women made me miss him. Not the thrill of the secret, or even the sex. As drippy as it sounds, I missed the way he kissed me, like we had been kissing for a hundred years. I craved the way he laughed, the idea that I could make him laugh. And this was probably one for my therapist—I missed the impossibility of pleasing him for the long term.

Now that the wife had taken her time inspecting our faces, she no longer knew what to do. The color left her cheeks. She turned away. Her ax-yielding assistant paced in front of us for a few moments, then you could almost see the idea light go on. She had a captive audience. Literally. She would treat this like a poetry reading. That's when it became really unbearable.

Her voice accelerated as she told how the wife would chop at the legs of our chairs; tear down the walls around us. The wife needed to see us all lopsided, exposed to the elements, foundations destroyed.

The youngest-looking one in the corner, with rings in her eyebrows, grunted out loud.

You're right, I wanted to tell her. He liked reasonably smart chicks so there was no need to simplify for us. We held some capacity for metaphor.

The ropes must burn, she said, burn, burn, burn!

As she went on, she seemed to grow bored with us. What a clusterfuck, she mumbled, between poetic declarations. She placed the ax by the door and kept talking. Likewise the wife dropped the whip and dug into her pocket for new pills.

I could no longer hear NPR. The things we take for granted. I missed NPR.

Quiet! the wife screamed from the corner, suddenly

aware of us again, back at it with the whip, a crack at no one in particular. She intended to be tough, but looked more like someone who needed to sob. I thought how exhausted she must be, how even in a short time he could exhaust a woman, leave her unsure of everyone around her.

She isn't going to hurt us because he isn't worth the trouble, someone behind me said. True, our crimes against her and her abduction of us—both gave him more power than he ever deserved. But for a long time I imagined he was worth the trouble. I would have never admitted it at the time, but I wanted both of us to screw up our current worlds and build a new and better one together. I had worked hard to get over him, to move onto new, healthier boyfriends. And it was hard to accept that I was still there, with him somehow, his past and present, stuck in the center of them all.

Finally ax-woman stopped with the poems. Back in the day, I had told my best friend Victoria that if I could talk to the wife I would tell her to get him an expensive Midtown haircut and a respectable black sports coat. Certainly I didn't mean to let him or his tarts off the hook, but it was easier to believe in his alleged bachelorhood with that Supercuts mop and an ill-fitting blue Brooks Brothers coat that had belonged to his dad. He was a gorgeous man, but one of those Panasonic nose hair trimmers would not have been a frivolous gift.

I thought he sucked in the sack, the kinky-haired girl sighed.

The wife dropped the whip harder this time and sat down again, yoga style this time, on the cement floor. She closed her eyes.

Wrong, I almost said. He was just older than he looked. He simply could not do what men our age could do—the balls could not keep up. That was the moment he seemed most human, when his dick was not working as quickly as he wanted it too; the moment we both became our frantic, imperfect selves. Sometimes he was brilliant in bed, but he had to calm down and find his groove.

Another one sneered: We're not exactly gathered to reminisce.

Or maybe we were. In my head I was still defending him—what the fuck?

Victoria always said, When men are amazing in bed, the odds are far greater they're gigantic assholes. I was tempted to disagree, but didn't have the right argument exactly.

At first he tried too hard; sex was more a marathon than an encounter. And he would sweat so much—maybe the others liked that—which made an immediate shower a necessity. I hated shower duets. When you shower together, someone is always left in the cold.

I tried to keep my mind off how much the ropes hurt.

The first and only two interrogations took place on the other side of the crates. The producer and the dermatologist, the kinky-haired girl told me later. The ax-poet stayed with the rest of us and blasted Aerosmith from a boom box so that we could not hear a thing. *Dream On.*

I suppose it was predictable. In the end, the wife broke down before she could finish interrogating everyone. So many things she only thought she wanted to know. The assistant-turned-ax-poet untied us and shoved us out onto the cold downtown street. She bitched that this whole scene was worse than *Law & Order* writers going on strike in the middle of the season. It wasn't an accurate depiction, but accessible on an otherwise confusing day.

It seems important to note that none of us imagined him—upon learning we were bound in a room with his wife, his wife breaking down—racing in for the rescue. None of us had seen him that way, ever, and knew better than to hope he had changed. He would not be there for us and he would fail her again.

Only the young one thought of pressing charges against the wife and the ax-poet when it was over. We all went back to our lives, now reminded of him by the sight of axes or whips, frayed ropes or wooden crates. In that way the wife had won. She had replaced any lingering thought of him with the memory of her eyes staring into ours.

The ax-poet wrote a book. The wife stayed married.

It was over, really.

Let me say it again: no one looked toward the door for him, not even for a second.

Acknowledgements

The author would like to thank the many people who helped this book to fruition.

Pam Houston, Amy G. Davis, Gina Frangello, and Allison C. Parker believed in my work from the beginning and set extraordinary examples with their own. Tammi Hayes-Guidi, Francine Matarazzo, and Laura Taylor Kung read early drafts of these stories with vibrant minds and open hearts. Tod Goldberg and Wendy Duren possessed the near-psychic ability to send exactly the right email at exactly the right moment.

I feel privileged to have studied with the late Bill Glavin at Syracuse University; Shawn Shifflett, Gary Johnson, Ann Hemenway, and Lynda Rutledge at Columbia College Chicago; and Aimee Bender at UCLA Extension.

The Radgale Foundation on two occasions provided me the precious gifts of writing time and community. I am grateful as well for many valuable work weeks in the summer program at the Fine Arts Work Center in Provincetown. I am indebted to the excellent team at Elephant Rock Books; Dan Prazer, Lee Nagan, Melissa Lucar, and especially my inspiring and wise publisher, Jotham Burrello.

I am humbled by and thankful for the love and insight of my family; my mother, Patricia Bierlein; my sister, Stephanie Bierlein; my beautifully precocious daughter Elliott, and her father, Edward Connolly.

Stories in this collection have appeared, sometimes in slightly different form, in the following literary magazines and anthologies:

"A Vacation on the Island of Ex-Boyfriends," in *Clackamas Literary Review, Fall/Winter 2003*

An excerpt from "Blink and Release Me," as "Gestures of Strangeness," in *SLS Literary Review.*

"Luxor," in *So to Speak: A Feminist Journal of Language and Art*, and subsequently in *Standards: An International Journal of Multicultural Studies*

"Men's Furnishings," as "Adulthood," in *Pearl: The 2003 Fiction Issue*

"Stalking Is a Dance," in *Clackamas Literary Review, Spring/Summer 2000*

"The Challenge of Acting Normal," in *The 2nd Hand*

The story "An Interrogation at the Prison of Ex-Girlfriends" was written for the 2008 Dzanc Write-a-Thon. www.dzancbooks.org.

The following stories were performed on stage in North Hollywood, California, in early 2001 as part of the New Short Fiction Series, under the direction of Sally Shore and Blonde and Brunette Productions in association with The Road Theater Company, Other Side of the Hill Productions, and the Los Angeles Department of Cultural Affairs:

"Luxor," performed by Julie Pop

"Stalking Is a Dance," performed by Kaci M. Fanin

"Traffic," performed by C.C. Pulitzer

The author gives special thanks to Kim Addonizio, whose story "In a Box Called Pleasure" is quoted here "In the Protection of Levees;" and to Kelly Link, whose story "Carnation, Lily, Lily, Rose" inspired the fictional short · film in "Three Naked Men." The story "In a Box Called Pleasure" appears in the collection *In a Box Called Pleasure* by Kim Addonizio (FC2, 1999). "Carnation, Lily, Lily, Rose" appears in *Stranger Things Happen* by Kelly Link (Small Beer Press, 2001).

a vacation on the
island
of ex-boyfriends

stacy bierlein

ELEPHANT
ROCK
BOOKS

A Reader's Guide

An Interview with Stacy Bierlein

Elephant Rock Books editor Dan Prazer spoke by phone with Stacy Bierlein from her Newport Coast office to discuss the process of writing *A Vacation on the Island of Ex-Boyfriends*.

Dan Prazer: It dawns on me that this has a very West Coast feel to it. How does where you are affect or inspire how you write?

Stacy Bierlein: I wrote most of these stories between 1998 and 2004, when I lived in Los Angeles. I had moved to Los Angeles from Chicago, and it's fair to say that one of the earliest stories in the book, "Stalking Is a Dance," is my love letter to Chicago. I always say that Chicago taught me how to get the emotional landscape onto the page. Chicago literature emerging in the 1990s had this extraordinary in-your-face realism. Then Los Angeles, a city that spills over its own boundaries, insisted I take stylistic risks, let the fantasy in. I had a neophyte's vision of Los Angeles, an admittedly idealistic one. It seemed like a place where anything could happen. If the Chicago literature I experienced in those years said "this is what one must face," Los Angeles literature said, "this is what one strives for." In 2005 I moved to Newport Coast, an hour-and-a-half south of Los Angeles. Three stories—

"Ten Reasons Not to Sleep With a Poet," "Where It Starts," and "An Interrogation at the Prison of Ex-Girlfriends"—were written in those first years outside of Los Angeles.

So yes, the places I live and discover have an unyielding effect on me, and it felt natural to pass those fascinations on to the characters in my stories. In the late 1990s and early 2000s I had the good fortune to travel in South Asia as well as Eastern Europe. I spent time in Nepal, traveling in and out of Kathmandu to Tibet and Bhutan. In Nepal I kept meeting Westerners who had just traveled the Golden Triangle, Thailand to Laos and Burma. The stories they told about Burma were amazing and affected me for a long time. Glimpses of these appear in the story "Traffic." The travelers I met in those days seemed to me changed by Burma's stunning contradictions—a land of great beauty in true political despair. If I had not previously been a writer, I would have become one listening to travelers' stories in Kathmandu.

Laura Taylor Kung, an elegant writer who was one of my first friends in Los Angeles, read many of my stories as works-in-progress and suggested that on these pages sexuality is treated like a voyage or landscape as well. Certainly I'm drawn to this idea. In a culture where our so-called leaders are constantly advocating for abstinence education, there is little discussion of sex as a means of self-exploration and self-examination. For the women in these stories, it often is.

DP: Where does it go from place? What's the next step that takes your attention?

SB: The stories live in my head for a while before I ever put them on the page. Once my mind's eye is settled in a place, I focus on the characters that inhabit it.

I have a seven-year-old daughter, and when she was younger she had an imaginary brother and sister, Ian and Emily. I delighted in her stories about them—they were so vibrant and fun. Ian wanted to go everywhere in his Spiderman pajamas. Emily did not care if the other girls liked purple and pink markers best; she was only going to use orange and yellow. At a parent-teacher conference in preschool I referred to my daughter as an only child and one of the teachers dropped her pen. The other jumped in quickly and asked, Who are Ian and Emily? I will admit my reaction to this moment may have been off-kilter. It was hard to suppress how pleased I felt that my little girl's fictions were so vivid and detailed they had fooled two adults who deal in make-believe every day. One of the teachers warned me, this is fine now, but if there are still imaginary friends at age six, you should be quite concerned. I adored both teachers—I envied their wisdom and patience; few people are so well equipped to teach very young children—and wanted to take seriously everything they said, but I was amused as well. I kept thinking, okay, I'm a fiction writer. I spend my days with imaginary people so I'm going to have a very hard time seeing this as a problem.

I share this anecdote because the women in my stories linger in my head for some time before I ever get them down on paper. In a sense, they become my imaginary friends. They are on my mind as I go to work and run errands, go about the tasks of daily life. I write in binges. I've never been really good at keeping a regular writing schedule. So while I'd love to say I'm one of those writers who writes every morning and for two hours after breakfast, that has never worked into my life and it's not the way I am inspired. So when, finally, that friend in my head becomes restless and has more details of her own than my head will contain, I get to one of those writing binges.

Before I started a family those binges could be amazing. I could lock myself in my apartment and turn my phone off and go for it. I could see the story through many drafts in a day or a weekend. "Men's Furnishings" and "Three Naked Men" are examples of stories that were created in single periods of writing hard. The stories that I've written more recently tend to happen in chunks, like "Where It Starts" and "Ten Reasons Not to Sleep with a Poet." I'll have only so much time to write until my daughter needs to be met at her dance class or my dog needs to be fed. My writing sessions have become less frequent but thankfully more intense.

DP: There's a very profound sense of loss throughout the book. Can you talk a bit about whether that's something that happened organically, or if that was something that occurred to you as you put the collection together?

SB: It's true. "Linguistics," "Three Naked Men," and "Two Girls" are most obviously about grief, but all of these stories deal in some way with the role of loss or potential loss in our lives. In the earliest versions of several stories, characters' sorrows were well masked by the excitement of new relationships or sexual encounters. In fact, a colleague who had read a few of my stories early on for a literary magazine worried that they might not work together in a story collection—that such a book could be too easily cast aside by critics as tales about women having sex in exotic places. And I thought, well, an author could do much worse than "women having sex in exotic places." Of course, the book is only about sex on the surface. Often the more important discussion is loss and how loss changes us. Another colleague said these stories are sexy and sad and that is an unusual combination. But I didn't think it was unusual at all. With every union there has to be an element of sadness for what's left behind, and with every new chapter there has to be some sense of losing the old one. To better answer your question: I really hadn't set out to write about grief. At first I tried to resist dealing with my own losses in my work, but at some point it became clear that grief was going to sneak in if I did not open the door.

DP: There are also themes of saving. In "Luxor," the narrator is saving the little girl, Mimi, and two characters are saving each other in "Linguistics." I noted the quote, "I am saving him from something the way he is saving me." Can you talk about that a little bit? It's the other side of the coin from the loss themes.

SB: I really believe that when you become aware of the role of grief in your life, you tend to connect with people who understand. In the year after my father died, I became closer to a friend in college who lost her mother when she was young. We were twenty-one years old and didn't realize immediately that we had bonded over that thing the character Vance ("In the Protection of Levees") calls "a deep inner sadness." We had coursework and dating and parties in common because we were meant to go about our day-to-day lives. But that friendship has endured and remained one of the most treasured parts of my life largely because we had that common emotional element. That was a core of our friendship, even when we weren't aware of it. And I like to think that true friends and lovers are always saving one another, even in the smallest of gestures.

In "Luxor" and "Linguistics" the main characters unite to rescue one another. But in other stories the notion of saving proved to be more precarious, and I experienced a fair degree of self-doubt in writing them. As a feminist, did I really want to put stories into the world where women suggest the right man can save them? Shouldn't these women be saving themselves? Yet these are not weak women. They are accomplished and determined and proud, yet vulnerable. My job was to make them tell their truths.

I thought about this recently, while revising "Where It Starts." My friend Gina Frangello, who is an extraordinary writer as well as my partner in my work at Other Voice Books, read the first draft of this story for me and recognized immediately that my heroine was swimming in a very non-politically-correct current. This is the story of a woman obsessed with a man who has to conquer women before he loves them. When the man in the story succumbs to a relationship, he leaves his younger female partner doing all the wanting—this is the best he can do. It creates an implicit dominance/submission in the story, and I liked the way Gina described that, calling it "emotional S&M." When the couple reunites, it indicates that this woman accepts she is totally abject before this man. This is not a happy ending, certainly, but the conclusion of her transformation—her surrender; her new willingness to be conquered. So in this particular instance the theme of saving turns on itself. To save her relationship, a woman will empty herself out, become ruined.

DP: Another story that comes to mind is "Two Girls." There's a consistency of success in one part of their lives, but not necessarily in their romantic relationships. I'm curious about that story in particular because I didn't see the violence at the end coming. How did that ending come about?

SB: The crime scene at the end was a surprise to me as well. For a long time, for many, many drafts, the story ended with two women looking in the boutique window, trying to look deeper inside. The story just kind of landed there, and it was a logical landing, but it wasn't a particularly comfortable landing for me. Perhaps it was simply too polite a moment to end on, too dreamy, so I had to muck that up. These are two women simultaneously conflicted by the events in their lives, but not shocked exactly; two women who have led sheltered lives in spite of their various successes. They lived in the right places and went to the right schools and excel in impressive careers. To leave them dwelling there without of some kind of push from the outside world seemed incorrect. I guess I felt I needed them to wake up a bit, and at first I didn't know exactly how to do it.

For my work at Other Voices Books, I was editing the

collection, *Simplify* by Tod Goldberg, as "Two Girls" was coming to fruition. Tod is an incredible writer, one who writes crime and violence with precision. I thought, here I am editing crime scenes and moderating writing conference panels about violence in fiction, and somehow I haven't really taken this dare in my own work. I wondered who the women in "Two Girls" would be in the face of a violent crime and then just sort of went with it. Early on, when I had written the description of the Amazonian woman on the beach, I hadn't had a plan for her demise. "Two Girls" had pushed beyond its intended frame.

DP: The two women in that story, too, they're photographing empty houses. That seems like that's something that on some level speaks to the larger collection. Everybody's searching for something. I'm curious to hear about "Linguistics." Where did the germ of that story come from, and can you take us through the revision and rewriting process for it?

SB: Searching and longing become important themes, and yes, I like "Linguistics" as an example of that. This probably isn't going to be particularly helpful for aspiring writers, but "Linguistics" is the result of a feverish dream. I was traveling alone when I starting writing it, staying in Prague after some time in St. Petersburg for Summer Literary Seminars. I had contracted giardiasis in Russia. My clothes were loose from the weight I had lost and I'd have these awful stomach cramps and at night I would have fevers. Those fevers came with vivid, strange dreams that would linger in my mind for hours in the morning. I had arrived in Prague late at night and went right to my hotel, dizzy with stomach pain and exhausted. The night fever came and with it this amazing dream where a Croatian man and I could not exactly talk to one another, but could not bear to leave each other either. I woke in my Prague hotel room with the dream still kind of spinning in my head. I made that room the setting for the first part of the story. But that night aside, I am not a particularly lucid dreamer. I've never before had a story emerge from a dream, but that one haunted me.

My time in Prague was too short so I continued the journey in literature. I read all kinds of things about Prague and clung to the details I wanted for "Linguistics"—the Charles Bridge and its pedestrian culture, the amazing tradition of puppetry and spectacle theater. For a while I wrote brief instances not sure how or if they would weave together. I have always been fascinated by language—by the way the arrangement and rearrangement of words in sentences can entirely change meanings, and in the ways we struggle to communicate when we are away from home. I went to Russia with only a traveler's guide knowledge of Russian. I had limited experience with the Cyrillic alphabet, but one of my best friends had been a Russian major in college and I had loved the sound and rhythm of the Russian language. Around that time also I had read accounts of extinct languages, and recalled a *Los Angeles Times* article reporting that one of the last speakers of the Native American Chumash language had passed away. Alice Parker, my friend Allison's mother, taught English as a second language and shared amazing stories of little intricacies in language that students would bring to her attention. So "Linguistics" morphed from a sexual dream to a celebration of language. It became an experiment in how much a story could hold. It took me dozens and dozens of drafts to get these instances onto the page in a way that started to make sense.

DP: Let's shift gears for a moment and talk about form. There are some stories that are nonlinear. There are some stylistic choices like not using quotation marks. As a reader, that slowed me down. What's behind that choice?

SB: I'm journalism-trained. I majored in journalism at Syracuse University and loved my coursework, but the temptation to make things up became overwhelming. I could stick to the facts but continually wanted to create stories to illustrate them. I thought, How am I going to make it as a journalist if already I feel stilled? My roommate at that time had written and published a stunning poem and encouraged me to write poetry. We started attending literary events at Syracuse and when those events inspired me to write fiction, I realized that was my true home as a writer. I think the story "Luxor" best illustrates that progression. I wrote an account of a terrorist attack at the temples of Luxor and could not resist an image of the Nile River—a waterway that is itself an enduring poem. Then the temples suggested the story of a woman longing for her child, and fiction took over.

The story "Luxor," because it emerged from a news report, did have quotation marks in early drafts. But as I crafted these stories, they felt to me so different from the nonfiction work I had done that I wanted them look different on the printed page too. I liked the idea of an aesthetic contrast between prose forms. Ideally, I wanted my stories to have as much in common with poetry and songwriting as nonfiction and memoir, and I wanted to express that visually; to find ways for them not to look like news magazine features. It occurred to me that writing without quotation marks was one way to do this, and for some of the more intimate stories, heavy punctuation simply felt too clunky anyway.

I thought there was an urgency and immediacy to the sentences without the quotation marks. So I decided I should try to get away with writing them that way. I looked to the authors who had done this and succeeded and they were legends—Amy Bloom and Alice Munro and Grace Paley—so that felt permission-giving. I wondered if I could stick to that stylistic choice throughout the book. So I experimented and liked the results. It wasn't a comfortable choice for every story; for many stories it was natural, for others I really had to play hard to make it work.

DP: And what about the nonlinear narratives?

SB: I'm not a particularly good linear thinker. I tend to write and think in fragments. When I begin a story I try to leave the associations loose between objects and events for as long as possible. When I crafted some of the passages that became the Crystal Cove cottage segments in "Two Girls," for example, I had been making brief notes about those cottages for some time. I had no idea when making those notes that the cottages would become a metaphor for fidelity. When I learned more about the fight to preserve Crystal Cove, I was drawn to the idea that these cottages were going to work into a story, but I had yet to know precisely what that story was.

I keep a fragment file, which is my version of a journal. I write descriptions of things that take my attention and save those in a file on my computer, trusting they will come out of the folder someday to find their way into stories. The result is that sometimes I organize stories in the way I recall those fragments, with less regard for chronological order or the passage of time. When I was a writer-in-residence at the Ragdale Foundation in Illinois, the visual artists there at the time were working in collage and I liked the idea that their processes had a good deal in common with mine. In fact, the story "Blink and Release Me" resulted from an actual collage I created in their studio by cutting and pasting segments of photographs and articles that had taken my attention. "Blink and Release Me" is linear, but it is chaotic in tone, and probably possesses more spontaneity than the other works.

In creative writing classrooms there is a lot of discussion of the reader-writer compact. What am I bringing to this story? What is the reader expecting of the story? In non-linear narratives there can be a very fine line between prose that is inviting to the reader and writing that threatens to distance the reader. Writing "Where It Starts," which moves backward in time, was an important exercise for me. "Traffic" is a story that needs to jump around in time. Margo remembers Nathan and Burma and her return to Los Angeles as her car inches forward in a Wilshire Boulevard traffic jam. The story needs to be mixed up somewhat to be true to Margo because in the moment of the story she is mixed up. The narrative would be less honest if an order were imposed on it. "In the Protection of Levees" is another story that needs to make liberal jumps in time and place to achieve its emotional truth.

The blessing of a story collection is that it comes together over several years time. The author has the space to experiment, to mix scenes up or rein them in. Stories might inform one another, or highlight and challenge each other. I think that's exciting.

Questions and Topics for Discussion

1. "A Vacation on the Island of Ex-Boyfriends" has a strong element of fantasy. How does this story set the tone for the rest of the collection?

2. "Luxor" is a fictional retelling of a real-life massacre. How does this contrast with the first story in terms of tone? How does the sense of place affect the characters as they deal with an unfolding terrorist attack?

3. Discuss Bierlein's treatment of timelines. Stories like "Where It Starts" turn conventional structure on its ear, moving backward in time, while others, like "Traffic," jump back and forth. "Ten Reasons Not To Sleep With a Poet" comes in the form of a list and has no chronological markers.

4. In "Linguistics," two people who have been recently hurt come together to find solace. What do they find in each other that binds them so tightly? When and why does it start to unravel?

5. Bierlein writes in "In the Protection Of Levees," the "tale of one broken family, at its core, is no different from that of the next." How does this statement echo throughout the collection?

6. There are stories throughout the collection that have strong metaphorical imagery. In "Stalking Is a Dance," the narrator and Jonathan, the object of her infatuation, both work as dot illustrators—of course, when you look too closely at pointillist images, they becomes simple arrangements of dots. In "Two Girls," the cottages are empty shells that people fight over. What other images took your attention? How do these images guide the reader toward the themes in the stories?

7. "Two Girls" is a story fraught with loss that ends with incredible violence. How do Tira and Page deal with the loss of their mothers? How do they balance the successes and failures in their lives? Does any of this prepare them for what occurs at the end of the story?

8. In "Men's Furnishings," Bierlein writes, "It's something like love, but even more complex." Discuss how this theme runs throughout the collection. What other characters run into a similar sense of complicated love?